Preface

The Love Buzz Anthology is a unique collection of poetry, lyrics, and short stories, by new writers.

Members of www.writebuzz.com were invited to submit compositions about love, in any of its guises, for inclusion in a printed anthology. www.arimapublishing.com kindly partnered writebuzz® in sponsoring the venture and co-produced the publication. This wonderfully creative compilation of 'love-bites' is the result.

The Love Buzz Anthology makes very interesting reading; it induces laughter, pulls at your heart-strings, and brings a tear to your eye - a bit like love actually.

Love holds no bounds .... *Lost love, found love, first love, forbidden love, tainted love, true love ....*

What does 'love' mean to you? Whatever the answer, you will probably be able to relate to many of the compositions in this diverse and inspired collection.

Are you a budding writer? Why not join www.writebuzz.com and become part of a dedicated writer's community. Please enter promotion code **Lovebuzz** during the registration process to qualify for a 20% discount.

arima publishing is a dynamic, niche publishing house catering for authors at all stages of their writing careers, offering both commercial and partnership publishing solutions including the specialised **new author programme**.

Dedication

This book is dedicated to: ....

With love from: ....

Message

Love Buzz Anthology

Sponsored by

and

Published 2008 by arima publishing

www.arimapublishing.com

ISBN 978 1 84549 303 5

© **writebuzz®** 2008, www.writebuzz.com

Printed and bound in the United Kingdom

Typeset in Palatino Linotype 11/14

arima publishing
ASK House, Northgate Avenue
Bury St Edmunds, Suffolk IP32 6BB
t: (+44) 01284 700321

www.arimapublishing.com

Ships (Legless)
By Adam Booth

How was I ?
Who was I?
Why was I
So very high?
Did we fly?
Did we try?
Did we soar
In space and sky?
Wish I could remember you
Where we are and what we do
Wish I could forever you
Wish I could forever
And do we like
What we do?
Think we might
Think we do
And do we fight
Or get blue?
Yeah that's right
Course we do
Ships that pass every day
Every night ships that pass
Ships that sink or float away
In the bottom of a glass
I wish I could remember you
Wish I knew the sense of you
Wish I could forever you
Wish I could forever

As
By Adam Booth

As I am

And want to be

The answer in

Your destiny

The indiscretion

You awake

The mercy for

Your one mistake

As I am

I always will

Calm you in

Your overkill

As you are

Will always be

The start of all

The end of me

LOVE
By Alwyn Gornall

Young love... delicate and fragile,
Like a spider's web.
Prone to be broken as easily
As a strand of gossamer thread.

Excitement and passion
Filling young ones' dreams.
A kiss freezing time,
For an eternity, it seems.

Mature love... soaring like the wind,
Powerful and free.
Beating in our hearts
Like the pounding of the sea.

As binding as an oath;
Held fast by the heart.
Two becoming one,
Wild horses cannot part.

The Wedding
By ANASTASIA Williams Cowper

As I began to get ready on our day,
all my nerves slowly drifted away.
There were only a few words that I wanted
to say, to you.
They were simply the words, "I DO".
As I travelled from one state
to another in a strange country
to proclaim my love for you,
the thoughts and feelings
I felt and the things I saw
no one will ever know how much
my heart and true feelings began to show.
The poverty all around me I did see,
from the little starving child
to that little mud house tree.
My wedding day was so special and so true
simply because, it was the Love we shared that
shined through and through.
When I saw you standing there next to me
my heart started to miss that odd beat.
I had the man of my dreams now standing at my feet.
That first kiss, that first cuddle, that first embrace
I will always treasure with so much dignity and grace.
I love you my darling with every beat of my heart.
My love for you has grown from the very start.

Love
By Barbara Peabody Pouliot

Love has no boundaries.

Love has no end.

It transforms with the beauty of life;

Bringing us closer to God with each and every

transformation.

Until one day,

We see God's face,

Embrace him,

And know;

LOVE IS FOREVER.

Love is the Freedom
By Barbara Peabody Pouliot

How can I truly love you,
If I don't truly know you.
How can I hold you,
If you don't let me near you
How can I see you,
If you don't look my way.
How can we talk,
If there's nothing to say.
Love is not a one-way street;
Two separate ways, with a separate pace.
Love is the special place we meet,
And recognize each others face.
No one ahead, No one behind,
Sharing the beautiful treasures we find.
All of the lessons we learn on our way,
Love is the freedom to live life each day.

To love you is to let you go
By BeccaD

If life had been good and life had been fair
we'd have been perfect for each other,
we would have settled down and tied the knot
and I'd be your children's Mother.

I would like to have shown you how much I cared
and what I felt for you,
but we knew we'd have to separate
and find somebody new.

It broke my heart to let you go
as it did time and time before,
each time we tried to say goodbye
we kept coming back for more.

But, now that we have been brave
and separated in this case,
knowing what we had would last
in another time, another place.

Don't go and change
By BeccaD

Say the right things - no, that just isn't you
and you never think of the things that you ought to
but, my love grows for you each and every day
and we are there for each other come what may

So don't go and change, at least not for me,
I give you my love unconditionally,
there's no place on Earth that I'd rather be,
than cuddled up to my love as he sits next to me

30 odd years and hardly a day spent apart
It's clear to see I love you, with all of my heart
and in a crowded room, we can still make eyes meet
Marrying you made me and my whole life complete

So don't go and change, at least not for me,
I give you my love unconditionally,
there's no place on Earth that I'd rather be,
than cuddled up to my love as he sits next to me

The vows we had taken were meant through and through
and I wear my ring proud as if shiny and new,
I love you so much and from our very first date,
I knew I had found my eternal soul mate

So don't go and change, at least not for me,
I give you my love unconditionally,
there's no place on Earth that I'd rather be,
than cuddled up to my love as he sits next to me

"Intercity Reminiscence"
By Bella Fortuna

Just a glimpse - just in time -
Of a place almost eradicated,
Though my memory
Has not yet faded.

Do you remember
(Of course you do)
That first tryst?
Lovers' penultimate kisses a-plenty...

Fuelled
By hot chocolate,
And secret promises.
The fulfilment of desire.

Soon the lovers' bower
Will no longer exist,
Flattened by Technology
In the hallowed name of Progress.

And we,
Once as one,
Are now
No more.

"Love is the Colour of Summer"
By Bella Fortuna

"Peacock" children are out to play,
Their antics make their parents' day.
Purples, pinks, yellows, and orange, too –
But what colour reflects if you're feeling Blue?

Green eyes and brown eyes pass me by,
Lipstick-red smiles, though some frown and sigh,
Stripes and checks full of colours bright –
But just how clear is the colour of Light?

Bright calm blue sky just for me,
It stretches as far as you can see.
Golden warmth from the sun above –
But just what hue is the colour of Love?

Sensation overload, it is clear,
Attacks each of us at this time of year.
Should one hide or flee, or stop and see?
Summer Love - the colour for you and me.

"Mr Molilino"
By Bella Fortuna

She was always bumping into him. They'd known each other for quite a while now. He was tall and slim, dark-haired and – unusual for an Italian, perhaps – green-eyed.

Francesco Molilino was pleasant to look at, if not drop-dead handsome. Smooth and suave, he was always impeccably dressed. Though he might not be super-wealthy, he had class and style. And he reminded her of a Lamborghini Miura; that beautiful car which was inspired by the unbeatable (at Le Mans) Ford GT40. A black Miura, naturally.

They were good friends, she and Mr Molilino – well, he'd rescued her from impossible situations on a number of occasions, and she was convinced their relationship was developing as it should.

True, there had not been a great deal to mention on the physical side (was he gay, all her friends wanted to know. As if that was the only explanation) apart from fleeting touches as soft as a downy breast feather from an eider duck. They really were such good friends, and emotionally intimate. Just like soul-mates, she thought.

Yet where was it all leading? Could their relationship be stuck in a time-warp, forever drifting in cyberspace? Not if she could help it.

When are we going to meet him, her friends enquired. Well, he might have a brother or a cousin. It wasn't easy for girls living in the big bad city to meet the perfect gentleman. Especially one who appeared to have some cash to spare.

So, she dreamed up another impossible situation and awaited her hero's attentions. Sure enough, he didn't fail her. And, having carried out the role of a chivalrous knight in shining armour, Francesco stooped slightly to claim his reward. His lips met hers as he held her tightly in that long-desired, long-awaited embrace. But then, much to her dismay, he began to fade – just like that poem Simon and Garfunkel had meant to write.

Waking in disappointment, she sighed sadly and sat up. Astoundingly, there on the bedside cabinet was the most beautiful bouquet, impeccably wrapped. Just like those really expensive ones you see in the flower shop at "One Aldwych". She read the accompanying card – "To my dear true love and soul-mate. Forever yours, FM". She sighed again, this time with such pleasure.

"A Warp in Time"
By Bella Fortuna

A warming sun is dawning in the sky,
A cool breeze cleanses my weary mind.
I'll think of you often before I die,
The sweetest love that ever materialised.

Laughter always lights your gentle face;
I like to see the crinkles around your eyes.
I listened intently to every word you spoke
And the unsaid words you cannot now revoke.

You know, as I do, that those unsaid words were true,
And you know my answers are hanging in the air -
Patiently
Waiting to be plucked,
Like sun-ripened fruit.
Grasped tightly,
Devoured ravenously,
They tell...

Of a love so exquisite it can bear the agony of parting
Because absence
Is just a blink of an eye
For the Universe,
Just a hiccup,
A warp in time.

"Do I Miss You?"
By Bella Fortuna

What a beautiful calm evening,
Even though it's raining now.
What a splendid day it's been,
Even though you did not share it with me.

What a memorable moment -
That golden gleam
From behind the edge of
All-encompassing dark cloud.

Do I miss you?
Does one yearn
For the return
Of the sun?

"Different World"
By Bella Fortuna

Today is gloomy, dark and dank;
The grey, stretching on forever, feels eternal.
Gentle drizzle transforms pavements
Into magical, mystical mirrors -
If you step out you
Might end up in a different world.

That's where I am now.
In the distance, a family of towers
Is shrouded in mist and mystery.
My soul feels the power of the
Encroaching Spring,
And my heart is as on fire
As a hot mid Summer's day...
Love takes you there
Even in English weather.

"The Accountant"
By Bella Fortuna

She'd always thought that accountants were boring, wore brown suits to prove their reluctance to try out new things, followed rules, ticked boxes and never laughed.

The man she'd met in the hotel said he was an accountant so, when he asked her out for a drink, she didn't hold out much hope for a night of steamy-hot passion or any other form of excitement, really.

Still, when you're all alone, in one of those big hotels indistinguishable from their competitors, in London, immediately after the break-up of a long-term relationship, even an accountant would do.

She couldn't face another night of telly, or staring at the décor in that bar where they all thought she was a hooker. That's the trouble with men, she thought. If you were on your own you were obviously looking for it.

He was easy on the eye, even if he didn't wear a brown suit. Since you ask, it was navy, with a sombre silk tie. He was kind of cute – big, innocent blue eyes surrounded by gorgeously long lashes that she'd have killed for. He had been smitten by her, or by lust, or maybe even lust for her. No matter; it was a good starting point.

He brazenly waited for her to order the champagne and charge it to her account before putting his hand on her knee and moving it slowly, seductively, up her leg to her thigh. At the same time he stared deeply into her eyes and his stare told her how beautiful she was. A fact she knew already. Her indistinguishable room beckoned to both of them.

The accountant neatly folded his clothes over the back of the chair and placed his mobile and keys in his shiny black shoes. Now entirely naked, she could admire his muscular frame and note that he was rather interested in the outcome of the evening. As, of course, was she.

The foreplay and the ball-game were as expected. Good, given how well he was endowed. The after-play was different; he didn't fall asleep straight away. No, he told her lots of jokes instead. They were not politically correct but they were funny. He wouldn't allow her to speak; he was captivated by her laughter. He was not the sort of accountant she'd expected and the night was far more entertaining than she had hoped for. Eventually, they slept.

When he awoke, the accountant had a desperate urge to pee and, as he stumbled to the bathroom, he realised she wasn't in her room. In fact, he wasn't in her room. And neither were his belongings. Hell, that wasn't funny.

She was sitting in First Class on the 5:27 from Paddington. She'd ditched most of his belongings, naturally, but the wallet had been intriguing. Made from beautifully soft leather, it was well-endowed, just like him. Or, so she had thought. It's amazing what you can do with old newspapers.

"I'm In The Mood For Love..."
By Bella Fortuna

I'm in the mood for love…
I think it happened when I looked above –
Saw the cool, golden moon eaten by an eclipse,
And wondered how things could come to this.

I'm in the mood for love…
Now powerful emotions are on the move;
My heart has swollen, there's no room to breathe
And something weird has happened to my knees.

I'm in the mood for love…
You've still got time to get into the groove!
A bud, glowing green in the warm sunshine,
Promised me faithfully you were mine.

I'm in the mood for love…
Don't let me down, simply behave
As though you were possessed by Cupid, too,
And gently whisper his magic – say: "I love you".

"Messages From Aurora"
By Bella Fortuna

For Iris

Message 1

Prince, I am waiting – what's taking you so long?
I sit and ponder; maybe something's gone wrong.
They promised you'd awaken me with a sweet, tender kiss,
That we'd spend our lives together, and cosily reminisce.

Message 2

I was certain real love had passed me by –
No longer would my lonely heart sigh
After someone so cute, so cool, so true,
And then, amazingly, along came you!

Meeting you has totally transformed my life –
You've brought me love, with a touch of strife.
Whereas before there was loneliness and peace,
Now its excitement tinged with bliss.

"The One"
By Bella Fortuna

It was just another ordinary day, really, although Isobel decided to have this one all to herself. If she had been clear in her thinking, she would have agreed that every day was a day to herself since he had left her and taken Snowy with him. How cruel could one man be?

Snowy had been their – her! - adorable Bichon Frise. But even if he had not taken Snowy, she remembered that Snowy didn't speak and, sometimes, Isobel craved the company of someone who did.

So she called Maria. They agreed to meet in Cafe Nero in Jubilee Place. After all, there was no point in having a day to yourself if you couldn't share the finer points of it later, with a friend. And Maria just loved a hot gossip. It would be a fun day, after all.

Isobel dressed. She loved that retro look and had recently invested in a pair of knee high black leather boots. She had been told that, when she wore them, she looked sensational. Yes, with the boots and the Ray Bans she knew she would look sensational today.

The weather was gorgeous – blue sky, marshmallow clouds, no wind – but it didn't matter. She was off to Canary Wharf, London's (as yet unacknowledged) third city. She loved shopping there. Gigantic glass towers housed two very pleasant shopping centres. She was going to make those till bells ring today.

A few hours later she was laden with designer shopping bags. It was too early to meet Maria but she needed some sustenance to keep her going. She thought she'd make her way to Carluccio's. "It" happened as she turned the corner by the HSBC bank. A young man walked, full-force, straight into her. He knocked her, her glasses and her shopping across the floor. Still dazed and in shock, she stared into the face of 'the one'.

'The one' was full of remorse. He helped her – "every so gently", she was to tell Maria later – to her feet. He gathered her belongings and guided her towards Carluccio's. He insisted he would buy her something – anything, perhaps their best hot chocolate? - as that would aid her recovery.

Isobel definitely desired hot chocolate. And anything else that would give her more time with 'the one', so she agreed. They drank hot chocolate whilst staring into the depths of each other's soul. Then he found her retrieved glasses, and passed them to her. She placed them on the end of her delicate, retrousse nose.

"And that was what did it", she confided in Maria. "When I put my glasses back on, I could see that, however deep his soul, he was not 'the one' after all. He was simply Ron Davies from Sales."

"Chicken Soup"
By Bella Fortuna

The world was a very different place when I was a child. Expressed in tones of sepia, and black and white B movies, young people then seemed even older than I am now. It was a world of small horizons, tinned soup and a dearth of choice.

For 'every day' there was soup, courtesy of the maker of 57 varieties. That always seemed to the 'child me' rather strange; I knew only of two varieties, tomato and oxtail. The oxtail had probably never seen an ox but it didn't matter that much because neither had I. It did mean, though, that my world was usually brightened by their fluorescent orange-red offering - made even more wholesome by my mother, with the addition of milk and butter.

If the truth were to be known she made the addition so the soup would be more likely to satisfy six of us. Poor mothers, with large families to feed, were – daily! – appreciative of, and amazed by, the wizardry and wonderment of the Son of Man. There was always plenty of bread in our house although my mother's budget rarely ran to fish (unless you counted fish fingers, which we had for tea as an occasional treat).

Of course, today my mother would be classified as a wicked degenerate. You see, she smoked: 'Golden Virginia', no less. Cigarettes staved off her hunger and that stretched the available food, allowing it to be spread even further amongst her children.

On very special days (such as recovering from a serious illness, or coming out of hospital) my mother demonstrated her love for me by serving 'it makes double the quantity' chicken soup. The soup was usually followed by a small square of vanilla ice-cream (Neapolitan was far too exciting, and too costly, for the poverty-stricken in the Sixties).

Maybe, it was the promise of ice-cream that made the soup so sumptuous even though, in appearance, it resembled a glutinous mass of pseudo-vomit. Despite its looks, it's thick, salty globules slipped down throats as easily as an oyster might today.

Sometimes you have to look back in order to understand more clearly why you are where you are now. And where am I? Well, you did say you loved me, didn't you? Shall we do the chicken soup before or during the foreplay? Makes such a warming, welcome change from all that chocolate and ice-cube love routine, don't you think…

"Yellow Bridge"
By Bella Fortuna

"Yellow Bridge", that haunting refrain,
Plays softly. Against the glass,
Gently tapping, the winter's rain
Arrives at last.

Voices hushed. Restaurant lights low.
My smile – you once said it lit my face –
Now has nowhere else to go.
I had made this place my home.

My love – like the glory of the rose –
Bloomed once, then died.
I fear, like you, it will not return.
Love's death I'll mourn.

Solitary now, my packed bag
Leans against the chair.
You're no longer there to speak
But your words remain, ever-circling inside my brain.

My heart is dead. It bleeds yet no blood was shed.
How could it end?
You said you cared yet you declared
You preferred me as your friend.

I accept.
If it was meant, it would have been so.
I shall cross that "Yellow Bridge" now;
Just reminiscing, then I'll go.

Offender
By Borin Manbat

No choking by chocolate

No cruel cut of flowers

For these would be treason

Against our state.

With counterfeit notes

Demanding honey with menaces

Loitering with intent to adore -

These be my petty love crimes.

Italian Reverie
By Carl Glover

My thoughts are overcome by seductive, and mildly hazy,
memories, which blush when reminiscing of those lazy
late afternoons sipping cappuccinos at the leisurely pace
intended, before they joined the fast-food menu race.
You joined me at my red and white check clothed table.
Would this become a ruby-lipped, allurement fable;
that you should choose this very spot, but then again why not?
Sheltered by a canopy, and the mid-day sun so very hot,
and our view, 'breath taking' doesn't take it in. Beguiling
mountains
in the distance, and here in this square, everywhere, flowers and
fountains.
Perfection, but for the hustle-bustle of shiny motor scooters
cruising by, handsome, dark-haired Italian boys, pressing on
their hooters
vying to get your attention, with you, still intent on dazzling me.
Butterflies dance in my heart. My senses awake in such a
reverie.

Shenanigans
By Carl Glover

Not me.
I couldn't have.
I loved you far too much.
Not that you didn't deserve it.
You did.

Out there.
For all to see.
Photos of you somehow
removed from their secret album
How so?

Not sure
that you can face
it, and how do I feel?
Sorry? I guess so. Life tends to
do this.

There's you
grovelling now,
tearful, fearful, ashamed.
Perhaps, or not, who knows, but you?
Are you?

It worked
Did you doubt it?
But I am unimpressed.
My attention was all yours - You
lost it.

Star in my eyes
By Carl Smith

You're a star in my eyes,
can't be no imitation,
that twinkles in my time and space,
beyond all limitations.

A Universal persona,
a galaxy of loveliness,
that launches Super-Nova's,
inside my pounding chest.

Amongst the countless billions more,
of endless constellations,
it seems you have an aurora,
that must have come from heaven.

Wherever you may shine,
however far away you are,
my thoughts for you are near and dear,
in my eyes you're a star.

Smile
By Carl Smith

Look at me and smile,
then smile again some more,
your smile it has a style,
I couldn't show the door.

Its presence has no pretence,
so authentic, genuine,
if it is fake and wicked,
let it fill me deep with sin.

Delightful, irresistible,
a sensory refreshment,
impossibly unlovable,
undeniably, oh so pleasant.

If I only knew your secret,
the way you smile, the way you do,
then you could feel the same as me,
each time I smiled at you.

The Wedding
By Carolyn Peters

Ribbons, petals, silk and lace.
Tearful eyes and smiling faces.
Top hats, waistcoats, cravats, braces.
Such a wonderful wedding day.

Bridesmaids, pageboys, the bride and groom,
Friends and family crowd the room.
The band play sentimental tunes.
Such a glorious wedding day.

Solemn vows, exchange of rings.
Toasts and speeches, someone sings.
A feast and banquet fit for kings.
Such a splendid wedding day.

Dancing, fooling, shrills of laughter.
The cake is cut, more speeches after.
The beginning of a whole new chapter.
Such a marvellous wedding day.

All too soon, it's getting late
but this will always be a date
to cherish and to celebrate.
Such a fabulous wedding day.

The bride's bouquet lands where it will
Giggles, blushes, what a thrill.
The honeymooners waving still
at the end of their perfect day.

Foetal Love
By Chibuzo Orjiekwe

Like two peas in a pod they sat staring at each other,

You could call them 'entities' but their similarities were uncanny,

The level of co-operation commendable; their tolerance indefatigable,

Changing position in mum's receptacle, without quarrel or commotion,

Toady 'peek-a-boo'; tomorrow 'I see you',

The echoes of their playfulness; the mischievous thumps of their feet,

Only served to put a wide smile on mum's rosy cheeks

And when mum decided to look through man's machination

They could be seen cuddling each other earning a lot of adoration

Entity A to entity B "I wish we were Siamese. That means we will be inseparable my heart and yours will be one",

But there was a stubborn vessel, which kinked as they played,

Entity B began to swell whilst A shrivelled to a prune,

With frantic little hands 'A' banged on the walls of mum's vessel "Quick mum there's a problem save B before he drowns,

There was chaos and commotion as mum rushed to the hospital, "don't worry little ones mum will never abandon you",

The surgeon was skilled; the operation a bit tricky

The knot in the vessel sealed; Entity B so thankful "I'll never forget you A for letting me live, your heart is my heart from now and forever";

"Thank you bro" said entity A the unfortunate twin, "I was supposed to come first but I will not despair. Play for both of us and live for us two, I'll be waiting for you. Tell mum I love her day after day and bring her flowers for both of us as often as you can",

"I love you my brother even though you're not here. I'll never forget you till the day that I die",

Mum cried with happiness and also despair; I knew she will miss me but hopefully not for long.

I so love my brother for the short time we shared; just a pity I could not tell him but I'll wait, yes I will.

Escape!!!
By Chibuzo Orjiekwe

I stared at her, a picture of despair

Caught in the melancholic clutches of premenstrual tension

A changeling who promised to be my retribution

Spewing out the utterances of a hormonally tainted mind

I stared at her and with a whoosh took flight……..I escaped

How was I to rekindle a love so precious, exorcise her demons
of damnation, and reboot her corrupted hard-drive?

How was I to salvage a ship marooned in an ocean so unkind?

Answer………..I escaped

Running as fast as the wind would carry me

Skipping past 'go' and forfeiting my £200

Buzzing like a bee in search of pollen

My quest certain; my desire sublime

I needed that chalice, infused with fragrant love juices

………………..I escaped

That potion which promised passions untold

Its mellifluous odour, a pheromone that caressed my virginal
brain

That woke up the animal in me and provided it with purpose

Yes, I yearned for that which healed from within
That clung to her female form, a recipe for temptation

I yearned to come forth like we did in the throes of passion

I yearned to............escape

Alas I settled at my destination

The place where I was to pick up my vestibule of love

My heart was thumping in unbridled anticipation and in a
cacophony of exasperation I yelled out.............escape
please!!!!

"Coming up sir!" the shop assistant replied

"You even get a £5 voucher to spend on whatever you desire. A
good choice I must say to pick Escape. It's timeless, emotive,
sentimental and potent."

Without a word I grabbed the object of my desire

Hurried towards the door, a bag of nerves and worse a flatulent
messiah

I'll put an end to her pain, recharge her batteries, and suppress
her hormonal tantrums

Just like in the old days when we first met, soaked in much
perspiration

............I'd escaped

"What is this 'Escape for men' are you mad, are you lame?"

"Are you trying to imply that I have grown a thick mane?"

"The shaving kit on valentine, the exfoliator on our anniversary"

"Is there any need for you to instil in me this hairy malady?"

...............I escaped

A mistake easily made, no not her the perfume

A fool yes I am but it was the thought that still counted

I'll redeem myself, oh yes, this time with something less confusing

Escape no I won't, maybe Kenzo, maybe Armani

Spotty Passion
By Chibuzo Orjiekwe

You wake up in the morning, yet another lover by your side
Keeping me away with your tablet-a-day and letting him caress
  your backside
Your vanity all-consuming; your infidelity all-destroying
You pick at me with your tweezers; how insensitive, how
  unkind
How could you be so superficial, believing my love for you is
  skin-deep?
I'll be with you at work, and at play and even on our wedding
  day
So there's no need to see the doctor, who loathes my pustular
  presence
Who calls me 'acne' with such malice and shouts out 'vulgaris'
We'll be together forever; in sickness and in health
Even when you become plastic Jane, disgusted with your
  newfound mane
I'll reappear without despair; no surgeon can usurp me
We're all-for-one and one-for-all, connected by fate and our love
  for fat cakes
Those creamy hot chocolates and late night binges
Only make me swell up; the size of fat peaches
I'll forever be your sweet pimple, that zit you can't wait to pick
For every time you conceal me, I'll be back ripe and larger than
  ever

Suitcase made of Love
By Clare Doherty

Love has packed her suitcase made of lavender and lace

She lined it with affection and stolen kisses from my face

And in among the kisses she scattered pieces of my heart

And covered them with feelings so as they would never part

The last thing that she took was all the hugs that I had given

She put them in her suitcase and tied them up with ribbon

Love left me in the night with her suitcase in her hand

I listened as her footsteps took her to another's land

MY LOVE FOR VALERIE
By Ernest Jackson

I gaze from our balcony on to the beautiful blue Aegean Sea, so calm it could be a sheet of clear glass. A plumb line of late afternoon sunlight shimmers across the unbroken surface, almost to my feet. A hard-earned morsel accidentally drops from the beak of one of the many beautiful, hovering seabirds and creates a ripple, spreading ever outwards, the only break on this vast expanse of water.

I liken the circles to the closeness of the people in my life. At the centre is my lovely wife, the first line belongs to my three kids and grandkids, then further out my only sister and her husband. Good friends follow and my long-gone parents, once at the centre, are no longer there but will always be in my memory. Everyone has a pool of circles that change as we go through life but we learn, often painfully, that the circles are not forever.

In the distance above a high cliff, I see square, flat-topped houses, their absolute whiteness reflecting on a background of clear blue sky. Way beneath is the interior of a massive crater and I visualize the blinding steam that was created as molten lava boiled the sea when they collided beneath the blackest sky. As the top was blown off the great volcano the sound reverberated around the whole Continent, the seas rushed into the fractured crater, and the romantics believe the legendary Atlantis was thus created. Centuries later, I know this place as Santorini and wonder at its beauty.

My wife and I are privileged to be amongst only 80 passengers on The Sea Goddess, a luxurious yacht, moored in this water- filled, seemingly bottomless, crater.

I lean on the enclosing beech-wood rail, close my eyes and feel the warm, afternoon sun beating through my white tuxedo. The salty smell of the sea and the intermittent screeches of the hovering seabirds take me back to my childhood on the Mersey waterfront. Oil-based smells of the docks and warehouses are now only in my memory, and I know it was unkind, and untrue, to say the most likely sound of the seagulls of Bootle would be a cough.

As I open my eyes and lift the crystal glass to my lips my thoughts are broken by a cheerful "Can you zip me up" and I move through the patio doors to see she is ready at last.

At five feet three, she is still slim and shapely with short, soft grey hair. Her taste is perfect, as usual, and tonight she wears a beautiful black, full-length dress with, of course, all the coordinated accessories. Her jewellery is unpretentious and perfect for the occasion. Her delicate perfume lingers, almost unnoticed.

I brush a fleck of glitter from her cheek, smile an unsaid "Lets go then", and we move out into the corridor, ready for a perfect evening to complete a perfect day. Forty years since we wed.

My heart is full of my love for Valerie.

An Anonymous Couple
By Hugh Hazelton

An anonymous couple: Sitting together either side of a small scissor-legged table over by the wall: Both in their mid fifties: She perhaps long ago beautiful, with short pale-ginger hair that perhaps, long ago, might have been flame red: He long legged and slender with sad, expressive grey eyes to match his hair. Around them the jubilee reunion party buzzes on unperturbed.

She smiles self consciously: "I'd quite forgotten how tall you are!"

He does the same: "Been the same height ever since I was seventeen!"

"I remember. It's ... strange meeting up again after so many years."

"Thirty-five years. I often wondered in our mid twenties what might have been if you and I could have met up again then."

"At the time we split my aunt wanted me to concentrate on my career. She'd been like a mother to me after all."

"And looking back on it now she was of course totally right. Your career is crucial, and stays with you for life. My father couldn't have cared less about me having one. Just wanted me gone. Did you get into midwifery as I remember you always saying you wanted to?"

"Not quite. Paediatric nursing. Till three years ago. Part time training job now. So tell me, are you married?"

"Yes. Twenty-seven years. One daughter."

"Thought I'd spied a wedding ring! Happy?"

"Yes. You?"

"Twice divorced! One son. He's nearly thirty now."

"You won't still be living at the flat then?"

"Well we did till twelve years ago. But when husband number two departed I had to sell up. Still in the same area though."

"I still remember the first time I ever saw you. Sitting on that bench in front of that window at that dance. Your hair was so red! Like a Titian beauty's! And then you looked up ..."

"I remember you coming over! I thought you were well dressed. And nicely spoken. We went to some folk club with some of the gang the following Saturday, didn't we?"

"Only time I've ever paid money to get into one!"

Silence. Finally he speaks again: Uncertainly: "Could I ...? Do you mind if I say something?"

She nods her ascent.

"I've nothing to gain - or loose - at this distance in being dishonest with you. All those years ago, I didn't have the eloquence to tell you properly then, but the feelings I had for you were real. I *never* thought of you as just some bird to get a leg over. I wanted you to know that. For all that it's worth now." A short pause: "All those years ago, even though we were just nineteen going on twenty, you really were loved. Truly. By me."

She smiles at him. "I know. And I've never quite stopped remembering you, either."

He leans back again in his seat, and she emulates the movement. "We can still be friends though?"

She smiles. "Oh, yes."

An anonymous couple ...

Beneath African Purple
By Hugh Hazelton

A supreme golden-yellow moon reigned high in a darkly purpled East African night sky. From all around came the constant rustle and chirrup of the countless trillions of tiny insect creatures paying their homage.

"The same moon, Monashia. The same moon we are seeing now, she shines in my country too."

Monashia had remained standing, her beautiful face, as ever framed by the mahogany coloured wig she so loved, a mere darker silhouette against the starry purple backdrop. She giggled: "But Dorsetshire is in Europe!"

"My country is England. Dorsetshire is a district."

"And why do you call the Moon 'She'? The Luyia people say the Sun and Moon were jealous brothers who fought over a beautiful maiden. They wrestled and the Moon fell into the mud. The Great Creator separated them, and ordered the Sun to shine by day, and the mud spattered Moon to illuminate the darkening world of witches and thieves!"

"The moon spins round the world, as the world spins round the sun. Never ending motion."

Monashia giggled again. Reginald already knew how much he adored the sound. "I know. I went to school in Mombasa till I was eleven, remember!"

Reginald reached out and took gentle hold of her freely hanging hand. She didn't pull away.

"In Dorsetshire the moon and stars are the realm of lovers. Beneath which a young man declares himself to the young woman he loves. Luna, the moon goddess, she favours lovers you see."

"And does this Luna truly believe that you truly love Monashia, Regin ... ald?"

Still she struggled with the pronunciation! "We could live in Dorsetshire some of the year, and the Moon could take your messages for you back to your family here." He disengaged his hand from Monashia's as she sat down upon the log beside him, and slipped his arm around her bare shoulders. Despite the chill of the African night her flesh felt warm still, and his gently caressing fingertips could detect the faint pelt like quality of her skin, smooth on the down stroke and slightly rough on the up.

"Pieter says he will make me 'a top model' and everyone will love me!"

"And where would Pieter take you? Amsterdam? Pass you around all those photographer chums of his?"

Reginald felt his heartbeat increasing as Monashia rested her slight weight against him. "Would you fight Pieter, Reginald?"

"If I had to. But it has to be your choice. Not the Great Creator's. Yours. No one else's."

Another giggle: "Pieter would wrestle Reginald into the mud I think!" The long, thoughtful sigh of Monaisha's exhaled breath intruded into the noisy silence. "Here is my place, Reginald."

Reginald considered for but a moment. And the fact that it took but a moment clinched it in itself! "Then I would make hearth with you here, Monashia. And the Moon can carry my messages, all the way to Dorsetshire."

"Hmm ..."

Two souls soared moonwards together as they tenderly kissed beneath a starry, African purple sky.

Slave to Fortune
By Hugh Hazelton

Her black skin artificially burnished with sticky coconut oil, she cowered within the sad huddle of slaves in the squalid, claustrophobic Cairo market. The trauma of her brutal theft from her father's village in Tigre, the chained march, and the long *dahabeyah* journey down the Nile had taken their mental toll. Likewise the meagre diet of *dourra* flour bread, the primitive sanitation, the lustful violations by the slave trader Ahmed and his vile Greek overseer.

But as the older women had explained, Abyssinian girls, widely famed for their great beauty, were a highly valued commodity in the harems of the Ottoman Empire to the north. And she was greatly more beautiful than most.

There seemed a commotion within the circling crowd. And then he appeared pushing through, the same tall, pale skinned man she'd seen watching her yesterday whom someone called 'Englishman'. Behind him scampered a scrawny Egyptian wearing one of their familiar red fezzes. She lowered her gaze as the Englishman stopped before her.

Ahmed, the Greek overseer, and two other guards sauntered over. Ahmed salaamed extravagantly. "*Effendi* ...!" The Egyptian began jabbering away in a rapid Arabic dialect she could barely follow. Grinning, Ahmed pushed his fingers inside her mouth and forced her jaws apart to display her fine teeth. Then he ripped open her white cotton garment to expose her dark breasts, making his familiar cackle as he began fondling her nipples. At once the Englishman's hands slapped Ahmed's away before carefully recovering her decency. She looked up into his clear, sky-blue eyes, registering with surprised astonishment what she plainly saw there.

More jabbering and bargaining. The Englishman was holding up five extended fingers in front of Ahmed's face. Arms aloft, Ahmed cackled. The Greek and the others grinned. Overlaying scents of cooked meat, spices, and sewage assailed her nostrils as the crowd started to become resentful of the tall infidel. A Coptic Christian, she prayed silently to her one true God.

Three dark haired Berber warriors carrying circular shields and wickedly long scimitars moved in behind the tall Englishman and his nervous Egyptian companion. The Englishman half turned and spread the flaps of his jacket to reveal the plain butts of two heavy calibre pistols nestling in cross-mounted leather holsters, their primed frizzens closed, their cocks pulled back to the half position. The Berbers snorted, shuffling their feet in the dust.

Ahmed emptied out the leather bag the Englishman had handed him into his palm, counted and re-counted the five gold guineas. Finally he slipped them inside his striped yellow robes.

The Englishman's arm was tightly around her shoulders in an instant. Then the three of them were backing cautiously away from the sullen, murmuring crowd. At the corner of the narrow street the Englishman tossed the Egyptian a silver coin, then took her hand as they sprinted through the bazaar and on towards the Mosque of Sultan al-Muayyad.

She squeezed his hand clasping hers. Slave no more, and never again would be!

The Princess of Yemen
By Hugh Hazelton

Kept securely rolled inside the flying carpet by day, Abdulla knew the magic stick would arouse no suspicion: A wondrous device, extendable, like the sloughed skin of a desert cobra, a transparent circular stone set in either end. "Herdsman, follow its vision every time the Flaming Orb sinks into the west," the indolent Prince Ali Ababwa had instructed. "Far, far to the south, across the sands of Arabia, beyond the Holy City of Medina, you must follow the vision and return my kidnapped betrothed unto me. With silver shall you be rewarded. And may mighty Allah protect you, for so it is written."

And so it came to pass that Abdulla the Herdsman had set out from the oasis of Majma'a, the flying carpet which was to be used to bring them back slung behind the camel's fine damasked leather saddle, and the magic stick concealed within it. And every dusk, before pitching his goat skin tent for another freezing night beneath the starry desert skies, Abdulla trained the magic stick as Prince Ali had taught him onto the southern horizon. And every dusk she came to him, an unimaginably beautiful girl at the farther end of the magic stick, staring tearfully out to the north from some far distant citadel rampart.

Until finally the failing light was lost altogether, and the vision faded, and Abdulla's secret dreams would begin.

Finally after countless adventures Abdulla and Prince Ali Ababwa's favourite camel, Hasan, drew up at the gates of the impoverished mud walled city of San'a. Posing as a foreign emissary in the fine clothes Prince Ali had loaned him for the purpose, Abdulla was soon able to bribe himself a private interview with the captive Princess Fatima. The magic carpet - 'a diplomatic gift' - along with the magic telescope still concealed within its folds, he carried up to her high apartments upon his own shoulder.

And such was her beauty, and the kindness of her fair eyes, and the ease of her manner, that poor Abdulla, dropping to his knees, found himself all but rendered speechless. "Your Highness, I come to take you back to your betrothed, Prince Ali Ababwa, who awaits you at the oasis of Majma'a, for so it is written. A flying carpet, Your Highness ..."

Smiling she held up a hand. "This I know, for as you say, so it is written. Many, many passages of the Silver Orb have I waited. But I bestow my love only upon him with the daring and courage and determination to fetch me out from this horrid place of unwelcome custody. Arise now good and noble Abdulla, and fly us from hence to my royal father's palace at Basrah."

And thus it was that Abdulla the Herdsman and the Princess Fatima married, and built a family of three fine and honourable sons, and three beautiful and dutiful daughters, and lived out their days in happy and loving contentment of one another ever more.

For so it was written ...

Green Eyes
By Hugh Hazelton

All around the pavement cafe table humanity flows and swirls by in the baking summer sun: But my eyes are glued exclusively on the stunningly attractive 41 year old redhead sitting opposite me. She of the shamrock coloured eyes, and the strong Belfast accent. Cassie, my ex-lover.

"So how long has it been with the new toy boy now then?" I enquire.

She gives me her full on heart warming, heart wrenching, smile. "Seven months now."

"And is he any good? Is he being faithful? I mean, at only 23 he's going to have a pretty powerful libido. And lots of pretty girls of his own age around."

She smiles again. To her credit ... "Rest assured he's getting all the nookie he can possibly handle! And, in his very own words, is loving every minute of it!"

"What, you're talking five times a night stuff?"

"Ha! A girl should be so lucky! We're not living together or anything. We're just girlfriend and boyfriend. We spend most weekends together and see each other a couple of evenings mid-week."

"And how long do you think he'll stay interested then? Eighteen years is a very big gap. Plus you tell me he's English."

Like me. I'm English. Like most people in England are English.

She offers another, softer smile. "A good long time I'm thinking."

"But he's just living out a young man's older woman fantasy! Can you really not see that?"

The first smile returns again. "Sure but a girl can dream on, can't she!"

"So what's his best number of times on the trot then?" Too late, the burning question is out now. I can still very well remember what ours was.

"None of your business!" Her smile all but fills her broad, handsome face. "But seeing as you ask I did, in an intimate moment, enquire of his own estimate a week or two back. He named a figure but then added: 'But that would be ordinarily. With you probably ...' and added on another two!"

I feel my stomach muscles starting to knot. "So what was his magic figure then?"

"Again, none of your business!" She looks up suddenly, as if some kind of sixth sense is at work within her. "And there he is now! And he has a taxi already and waiting too. There's true love for you now!"

Her pronunciation of 'now' – "nuy" – lingers in my mind as she gets up and makes her departure.

"It's been grand. We must meet up for coffee again some time!"

I watch her move out into the throng of pedestrians, her tall, substantial form quickly lost to view. 'Cassie, wait!' I want to cry out, but no sound comes. Absently I glance at my watch. I'm running late. My son is playing in a school cricket match this afternoon and is going to need picking up. With my thoughts still very much elsewhere I flip open my mobile to call my husband.

Falling ...
By Hugh Hazelton

It was a bit like in that film 'Prime' I suppose. 'Cept it happened ten years ago. I was 'customer reception' at that exhaust centre which took over the old Pilot cinema for a time, and Jamie came to work there doing the parts bins. Twenty, just been kicked out by his step-dad, and me thirty-six! I was a bottle blonde even then, although back then my most obvious assets were a bit more gravity defiant!

He had this sweet innocence about him. Quite shy with an honest niceness if you follow me? And I guess in a way it was that which just so annoyed me! I was fed up with my then partner Mike's constant cheating and wanted to hit back at him, fed up with my lousy job in that horrible place, fed up with my whole life really. And so for totally the wrong, bad reasons I went for it. Came onto him real strong right from his very first day! The poor boy stood no chance!

Well, we certainly enjoyed one another as people as I believe the expression goes, until a couple of months in something very unexpected happened. It was a wet Sunday in April, and I'd gone round to his bedsit. It was pretty awful. We'd gone to bed - it was an old divan with a vaguely niffy duvet on it the particular aroma of which I can still recall - and we're lying tangled up like a pair of purring kittens in a basket following our third good shag of the day when all of a sudden he just spits it out:

"Gemma, I have to tell you this. I think I'm falling in love."

For a moment I'm gobsmacked! Outside the rain is blattering harder than ever against the leaky old sash window. Heavy beat music is thumping away from somewhere on the floor above. And then I realise it too. "Yeah, you're not the only one!"

So I dumped Mike once and for all, got myself a new flat, and eight weeks later me and Jamie wed! The fitters from the exhaust centre all came and gave us a crystal glass punch bowl and a microwave oven. And at the very last minute Jamie's mum agreed to come to the ceremony. And then just to really top everything I fell pregnant with Katie on honeymoon! I'd all but given up hope of having kids by then, so maybe falling in love improves your fertility too!

And now? Ten years on we're a happy, loving, contented family of three. I supported us so's Jamie could go through college. Katie was little then, so it wasn't an easy time. But we got through it and he's a qualified mechanic now. And me and Jamie and a sixteen year age gap? Hand in hand we're still falling! It's been an amazing journey. And d'you know what? It's still continuing and I don't ever want to stop!

The Judgement of Paris
By Hugh Hazelton

I guess I must be living out every forty something man's dream: To have to choose between two equally attractive younger lovers. Perhaps it is just my luck. Or my fate? But just as for that mythical Trojan prince whose choosing of Aphrodite's gift of Helen over the power of Hera or the wisdom of Athena ultimately precipitated the Trojan War, choice there has to be if love is to truly take root and flourish as it should.

And at least here that choice is down to just two goddesses only.

Wendy: The supermarket checkout girl. Just 24. Two kids by different fathers, long 'wet look ' blonde hair, petite body, extended happy family, and the face of a nymphet. Boundlessly cheerful enthusiasm for the kitchier side of life: T.V. soap operas, car boot sales, Siamese cats, house plants. And yes, for the other too! Like the time I'd bailed her brother out from the loan sharks. Such a thank you she gave me! And her mum, knocking on the bedroom door after three hours or so and coming in bright eyed and beaming with a tray of sandwiches and another bottle of vino: "Just thought you two love birds might fancy a bit o' light refreshment! Be back to clear way in twenty minutes then you can carry on!" Youngest teenage sister's grinning face peeking round the door ...

Nicolette: Thirty-eight next month. Human Resources Manager, and art lover. Lush dark hair with eyes to match. Picasso and Dali prints adorning the bedroom walls. Florentine guide book placed beside the bedside lamp. So well travelled! And shared late Sunday morning breakfasts of best quality marmalade on toast whilst sitting on pea green Lloyd Loom chairs in a sun warmed conservatory pretending to glance at the Sunday colour supplements. Concerts and recitals. Loves obscure Baroque composers especially. Ever heard of Domenico Cimarosa? His music could give George Fredrick H's a fair run for its money any day. Well, her mother was with the Halle strings section for a time in the '70's after all! Hours spent idly exploring continental art galleries, guide book in one hand, and mine in the other. Easy, relaxed, no need for unnecessary distraction ...

Paris, help me out here mate! For just as you handed your Golden Apple to your chosen winner, so I must now make the Golden Phone Call to mine! It is time, and decision cannot be deferred for any longer. And if that sounds horribly arrogant, please be assured that it is not meant to be.

It's ringing now ...

"Hi yourself! It's me! I have something very important to say to you Wendy ..."

Love on The Bay
By Hugh of Avalon

Tyrannosaurus Rex fossilized collar bone,
Or a signed sexy photo of Ms Sharon Stone,
Inflating bed dolly made in far off Mandalay,
Framed King Kong poster starring gorgeous Fay Wray ...

And I found all of them ... all ... on The Bay!

My whole life is filled with such complete, total crap,
That's been all lovingly posted, in double bubble wrap,
Something turns up here 'most every single day,
Stuff folk such as you would most like throw away ...

Seven Day Listings ... on The Bay!

Tell me why ... I just bought a street map of Nairobi,
Off some guy in Leeds, calls himself: 'Jugman Toby'?
'Cos when I checked out his Seller's Other Item,
I found he's another ... and that one's of Brighton!

I'd soon lose my way ... off The Bay!

A 'thirty-eight Beano featuring that man Desperate Dan,
Or a used Kleenex tissue dropped by Princess Anne,
Ffestiniog track plans drawn by James Swinton Spooner,
Or a Tata truck - tatty - built '96 out in Poona ...

You can flog dead horses sooner ... on The Bay!

Wanna buy ... sepia postcards of pre-war Belgian churches?
Or a rubber skinned blonde who sits up ... straddles ... and
   perches ...?
Or at least so it claims, in the Item Description,
And don't you just love the graphic photo depiction ...!

Getting down all the way ... on The Bay!

Now let's hit the Search button ... for something quite silly,
Maybe find Tutankhamen his long since lost willie ...?
Ask the Seller a Question 'bout those used black thong strings?
No they most certainly won't snap "with ear splitting pings!"

Unlike that surgical stay ... from The Bay ...

Cash, personal cheque ... or even card plastic,
I'll pay you at once, with a speed light fantastic!
You can't post her from Oslo? Well you didn't explain so ...
'Christmas Fairy with Halo: Arrange pickup from Tromso.'

Little tiffs make your day ... on The Bay!

Now just check out the score of my Feedback on here!
It heading right out through the high stratosphere!
All A ++++ Positive, One Hundred Per Cent!
A record, memento, of the thousands ill spent ...

A global world's Love, to me daily it's sent ... by The Bay!

And now my new found Love ... videoed dancer Roxana,
Or maybe her friends? Katriana ... Olga ... Tatiana ...?
I'm Winning Bid current on three out of the four,
So why settle on one when The Bay has lots more ...!!!

Oh I am so greatly in Love ... with The Bay!

Memories Linger On
By Jack Beeton

The evening dew surrounds me

Stars so brightly glow above

No clouds to hide the softest Moon

A summer night for making love

But no one there to hold me close

Or whisper tenderly;

Just a dream of yesterday

Always in my memory

Our Saturdays
By Jack Beeton

How little things in life meant so much to me
Without you here to share them I now begin to see
Never really liked the shopping at week-ends
But how nice it was to come home still the best of friends
We'd have our tea watch tele and talk awhile
Always time we had to share a smile
Sometimes with a prayer and a lot of luck
A blouse or skirt you would have picked up
You'd try it on, swirl around the floor and then try to improve it
So out the scissors came and with a little effort
The opening would be much longer and I was left to sew it
To the club we'd go so proud I was to be with you
I so much wish I'd made more fuss, as so often I wanted to
A romantic I never was, never showed much charm
But would always walk along with you so tightly on my arm
My love was there you did know this
But words to say how much, I know you must have missed
Again too late or may be not for you to hear these words I say
For only you now know the truth if we will meet again one day

The Gift
By Jan Miklaszewicz

the cartridges came separate all wrapped up in a pale brown paper that felt smooth to the touch. it was folded over so neat and crisp like origami. the thing itself was densely weighted and stole heat from the hands. a clinical piece of engineered ice. and its case was beautifully made. there were precise compartments and everything slotted in with a pneumatic sigh, the wrapped cartridges too. the manufacturer had even been so considerate as to provide a gently rolled up lint cleaning cloth.

when she had conveyed it to her home, so protective she let no one see, she laid the case on the bedspread and traced her fingers over its lines. she hoped he would love it. she knew how he suffered for his cause and it just seemed like the most perfect gift. nobody else would have been so thoughtful. certainly none of those other sluts.

his eyes went opaque when she gave it to him that evening. she took it for surprise. he was sitting at the table as he often did, a drift of cigarette ash over propaganda pages. his smile was small and straight like a coin slot. they did not make love.

when she left he opened the desk drawer and put her gift with all the other pens he had been given over the years and began to calculate how he would leave her.

Love At Last
By Jan Miklaszewicz

he was all she had ever wanted, would never let her down,
needed her you see. god you'd never known such a sweet
feeling as they lay there, him nuzzled against her breast, her half
asleep. there had been others of course. what woman could say
she'd never held another, never comforted, never whispered her
undying love. but this was it. she'd knelt before him, endured
his silly rages, excused his behaviour when her friends had
disapproved. and there it was. he was hers and she his. she
prepared meals for him and he refused the arms of others. bliss.
always glad to see her, never the recriminating questions of
where you been and who you seen. this was love. she'd found it
at last. as they lay there in the softness of her bed, he looked at
her. his face took on a serious aspect. she began to worry. what
was it? suddenly he began to cry. she understood. he needed
changing.

Famished
By Jan Miklaszewicz

rapunzel was love
and snow white too
even the A-team had some

rocky punched frozen meat
and got love
and it was ever present
but in my house

it got held
in front of me
in the same way
as does the home
and the job
and the lounging cats
that we give earthy names
and laugh at in blurry contentedness
when they look at us so disapprovingly
and purr

and
much like those dream laden cats
I stalked love
and waited
and hoped

and much like those marmalade cats
I found love
and caught love

and much like those cats
through the back door I dragged love
and much like those cats I was lost

and I looked to the owner
with disdain
and I looked at the owner
with bitter displeasure

for I'd broken its wings
and it didn't taste good
and I slunk
unrequited
and famished

Awake
By Jan Miklaszewicz

shaved her hair with a razor comb
and her eyes remind me of someone
I'd sooner not be reminded of
and it keeps me awake

and the thin shape
of her ass makes me sick
but I'd touch it if she asked me
and just the thought of it keeps me awake

she looked at me aloof
and the flakes from her pastry
stuck to her lip
and I hate her cos she keeps me awake

and I never heard her talk
though I imagined it sometimes
but it was like speak in a dream
and I don't do that cos I'm awake

and her eyes remind me
of some earrings I bought
when I was thinking about her
but fucking someone else

and when my she put them on
I took her to bed
and looked at them as I came
and I didn't sleep then either

I would kill her if she touched me
or more likely kill myself
oh yes I hate her
yes I hate her
cos she keeps me awake

The Man Door
By Jan Miklaszewicz

god that's fucking weird - why?

I don't know really - it keeps her happy

does it keep you happy? it's not right mate - it's fucking weird -
you're off your head

forget I said it - it's no big deal

have you done this with any of the others? it's fucking weird
mate

not before - no - anyway leave it alone will you

what makes her so special?

I love her

she's got you going round on all fours mate - you've even got a
fucking cat flap

it's a man door

whatever - you call that love? it's weird if you ask me

I didn't ask you

she can't love you if she makes you do that

but I love her

Love in the hand
By Jan Miklaszewicz

you speak of love as though it's a thing

could be cut from a bough

or detained in a cell

but it can't

a picked blossom will die

or bloom on another's vine

without the laughter of children

a playground is a carpark

and love in the hand

is nothing but sand

Devotion
By Jan Miklaszewicz

Hidden cicadas rasp the sky with noise. A dust road winds away from home and a wagon jolts with every pothole. Shame faced, he plots a way out.

She bears witness as a murder of crows is swallowed by the sun. The land is as flat as a lake here and heat rises from it in corrugated waves. The purple mountains beyond are distorted. Tasting a drop of sweat from her lip she sighs and goes into the shade.

She would throw herself into the void should he not return. Of this he is quite sure. She would be found hanged from a bough by the brook. Only twice per month does he leave her, and she is bitter for days beforehand. Maybe it's from childhood. Reality breaks down when she gets nervous. Things happen.

He has shrugged off her love like the snake his skin. Of this she is quite sure. It's in his face when he returns. In the way he won't meet her look. Every market day seems as though it's the last. This is a little game of his, toying her along, waiting. A cruel game. Clouds begin to creep across the sun.

He has loosed his bonds and is ready. Time microscopes down until every scrape of every cicada wing is separate. The guard is toppled, his horse goes wild, a sword falls to the ground. He makes a desperate lunge for freedom.

She should never have trusted him. Men are alike - their idea of love holds no trace of devotion. Just duty. The day squeezes in around her. The animals are lying down and the sun squints through blacking clouds. All she can think is betrayal and her despair feeds on it. Her lip bleeds where she has been worrying at it. She goes to the barn for rope.

He waits beneath the dapples of a black cedar tree. The journey had seemed short. As he suspected, she is making her way alongside the rill to where the trees overhang the water. This was the place they first met, a place where if he closes his eyes he can forever see and hear and smell her as she once was.

He skulks beneath the cover of the black cedar shadows. The day has been horridly long. Relief is in her, but so too is rage and she cannot keep the hurt from her voice. Her hands shake. She asks him where he has been and does not listen for his answer. She tells him he has betrayed her; that he knows neither love nor devotion. He tells her he is sorry.

Eventually he fades into the shadows. Fourteen miles away, a militia guard winces as his arm is slung. One of his companions looks to the body slumped double on the dust road. He removes the blade that the prisoner has driven through himself. The cicadas fall silent. The ghost is free.

Dinner for Two
By Jan Miklaszewicz

INGREDIENTEN: 1 lonely person, 1 lost person, internet hook up, time, boredom, time, obsession, time, masturbation, meeting, laughter (add alcohol to taste), mutual ignorance, shared superficial liking for something crap (perhaps head massage, or Orwell).

COOKENTRUXEN: mix ingredienten by thorough needing, rest in close environment without shade, apply heat (at this point add skeletons from closet), allow to simmer, stand until cold.

SERVENTUMSTRAUSS: gain unwanted baggage, achieve debt, swallow.

Poor Old Lambkin
By Jan Miklaszewicz

Poor old Lambkin built a ship
with timbers from his mother's lip
and tar squeezed out of fairy tales
and telly screens and such;
a mainsail woven out of guff
from magazines and horoscopes
and ropes spun out of grandma's hopes;
a mast of looking glass.
Out to the Sea of Love he sailed
and as at last he sunk the land
behind that slender frail stern,
the plan he'd planned got out of hand:
not another sail to see
but creatures risen from the deep,
deformed, lopsided, overbearing,
scaly buggers (monstrous beaks).
Some enraged at lovers past
spat caustic bile upon the mast.
Others cowed by vicious exes
screamed down from their crucifixes.
Frigid monsters (icy breath)
did huff and puff to speed his death
and randy ones with virus loins
rained warts the size of cannon balls.

Lambkin bravely fought the fight,
the sea got savage, day got night:
a crimson crash of menstrual blood
had caused the hold to fill and flood,
and when a blast of steroid cream
did rent his vessel down the beam
he plunged into the murky still
already thirty (and quite ill).

Heavy Heart
By Jason Minty

Heavy heart
Lump of lead
All gone wrong
Scrambled head
Feeling pain
Very down
No direction
Such a clown
Should have known
On the cards
Craving pleasure
Loss hits hard
Heavy heart
Lump of lead
All gone wrong
Scrambled head
Fell in love
Head over heels
Wooed the girl
Romantic spiel
Couldn't sleep
Lived the dream
She didn't feel
The same it seems
Heavy heart
Lump of lead
All gone wrong
Scrambled head

Witch Bitch
By Jason Minty

Too many bitches have I known.
I'm now resolved to spend time alone.
The last one, a cracker, just wouldn't go home,
And believe me I was scared.

Too many witches have I known.
I'm now resolved to spend time alone.
I still dwell on a beauty with an empty head,
Painful conversation, and needy in bed.

Too many bitches have I known.
I'm now resolved to spend time alone.
I can't forget Sue, who give her due,
foretold that she dreamt of babies.

Too many witches have I known.
I'm now resolved to spend time alone.
Anne was a man, I swear it,
she stole my wallet and I couldn't bear it.

Too many bitches have I known.
I'm now resolved to spend time alone.
The last one, a cracker, just wouldn't go home.
And believe me I was scared.

Game On
By Jason Minty

She's in a different league
(I bet you're gonna laugh)
She's in a different league
and she's crossed my path.
She's in a different league
Another psychopath?
I really hope not, this time.

She's in a different league
You know she likes to talk
She's in a different league
She suggested going a walk
She's in a different league
She could be my sister
But she's not, she turns me on.

She's in a different league
Forget the World Cup
She's in a different league
I'm giving everything (but her) up
She's in a different league
Keep your fingers crossed
It could work out, she's hot.

The Battle
By Jayne Kelly

This isn't a war
Yet I still need to fight
These words hold my feelings
That's why they don't read right

My heart is the battlefield
These words my ammunition
Though I can't find the right ones
Amongst all this confusion

I try to come out shooting
I don't want to come off worse
There's no healing for my wounds
I have to live by this curse

I put up my defences
Awaiting your attack
You'll try to break them down
The moment I turn my back

Although I know I stand to lose
It's all I'm able to do
Although I know I'm being used
I still want to surrender to you

It ain't that easy
By Jayne Kelly

It wears me out
It tears my insides out
There's a hole inside me
Still filled with doubt
These feelings don't come for free
It ain't that easy
To fall in love with me

I'm not sure what feelings I now own
There's always this emptiness of feeling alone
You say that I can talk to you
Though there's not much to say
When all your hope is gone
Words don't come that easy
It's hard falling in love with me

Look into me if you like
I have nothing left to show
All truth abandoned me
A long time ago
Look through me if you like
You'll notice I hardly exist
I'm not really alive
No matter how hard you insist
It ain't that easy
Falling in love with me

I won't encourage you to fall for me
I'll give you nothing in return
My soul is whole, my heart empty
There's a lot left for you to learn
It just ain't that easy
Trying to fall in love with me

Infidelity
By Joe Barrett

Unfaithfulness in a relationship is widely considered to be the worst kind of betrayal and few would argue that it isn't. It would seem that one of the main reasons for being in a relationship is to have exclusive rights to the romantic and physical love of our partner. It is clear from the vows and promises that we make and demand from each other that faithfulness is considered to be a signed contract in the domain of love but the questions remain: is it possible to still be morally right to dishonour this agreement? Are there any moral loopholes in this 'contract of love'? Can infidelity ever be justified?

Possibly the main justification of 'cheating' is if the offending spouse has also been betrayed in this way by the person he is cheating on. Our innate desire for justice tempts us to condone the act under these circumstances. Whilst our temptation to excuse infidelity in these situations may be understandable, it is not rational. Basically this is nothing less than 'two wrongs make a right' mentality that denies the worth of the 'contract of love' that they are using to justify their actions. This argument is inconsistent. A similar argument is if a spouse is somehow being neglected or abused by the other, that they are then free to act equally immoral. Likewise, instead of justifying bad behaviour, this argument condemns it by stating that immoral behaviour should not go unpunished. So, if the 'eye for an eye' philosophy only serves to convey the wrongness of infidelity, is there any other philosophy that could possibly justify it?

We have seen how the 'eye for an eye' attitude fails to defend the cheater against the charge of immorality but we can learn something from its flaws. This argument failed because it held as its main defence that infidelity is unethical. So, it would seem, the only way to effectively defend infidelity against the accusations of immorality is to attack the argument at its very root. As has already been stated, most marriages and romantic relationships are built on the foundation of trust and duty. The vows we make to each other are almost always taken with sincerity, they are born of the human need to know and control the future. However, it could be argued that the pact of mutual fidelity is unrealistic and naïve. Let us now take a closer look at exactly what is involved in such oaths.

To vow to do something in the future is much more than just promising to perform a certain act, it is swearing to 'be' a particular personality. Human beings have a tendency to change (sometimes fundamentally) over time and many consider this a 'good thing'. Our ability to grow and develop with age often leaves us unrecognisable from our former selves. It is feasible that because of this tendency, vows and oaths aren't worth the breath used to utter them.

Okay, maybe using identity theory to justify unfaithfulness is a little audacious but possibly no more than the quixotic expectancy of romantic love. Modern morality would probably place the rights of the individual above any ethic concerned solely with social moral debt. This philosophy sets the individual free to explore his/her existence without any obligation to anyone else. This belief may seem more like decline than it does progress but it is probably the closest we will come to justifying the self-absorbed act of infidelity.

Gone
By Joe Barrett

I miss who you were yesterday,

your smile, contagious.

Young, strong and passionate

about yourself and mine.

When your spirit was light it floated

free from the heavy anchor

that comes via maturity.

You were once beautiful

but not today.

And so I often sit in the hazy glow of nostalgia

of an already set sun.

For yesterday you were beautiful,

but not today.

The Prodigal Heart
By Joe Barrett

Through fear of carrying her stench,
I wash my face
and genitals in the sink.
For a shower could fuel suspicious minds

Clothed in a cloak of nonchalance,
Because I love you my darling.
You need not know my weakness, folly.
And love demands I protect you.

Already She is out of mind,
My heart she cannot know.
For yours it is, and has always been
No other can claim the heart of me.

Beside your soft skin at last my love
Your hair my comfort and my joy
Forgiveness whispered under breath
And our fingers entwined in proof.

And lust has no commandment now
My flesh is deaf to its call
Your breast is a refuge from Jezebel's gaze
Sleep well my Darling, My love.

My Childhood Sweetheart Wife is Leaving Me
By Joe Barrett

See ya babe

I love you, and I'm proud of you

you've done alright.

I'll be ok

sshhh

A Recipe for Love
By Joe Barrett

I made love last night

I read the recipe wrong though, and put in salt instead of sugar

Tasted ok though

And what do I know?
By Jools Coggon

Without love life remains wanting.
Nothing is as necessary - predictably.
Love is indefinable yet defines us.
When you give too much it self-destructs.
When you hold back nothing happens.

Love is about closeness and about distance.
Too intense and it suffocates.
Too remote and it's negligent.
Love only survives when nurtured.
Love needs reciprocation.

Love, all too often, is used as an excuse.
Reckless 'love' can lead to madness.
Fickle 'love' can turn to hate.
Feigned 'love' causes damage.
Lust as 'love' can't compensate.

Most of us sabotage love at some point.
Many of us crave love at some level.
Some of us let love slip between our fingers,
And others carelessly throw it away.

Hey, do I sound as if I'm wise?
Do I give the impression that I know where 'it's at'?
Not so.
I'm one of you who haven't got a clue.
But maybe there's a difference?
... I'm also one who'd really like to know...
Love.

The Wynding
By Jools Coggon

This feels good,
it's all that dreams
are made of .. then more.

This feels good,
it's somewhere that
we haven't been before.

This feels good,
it's wrap us up in fluffy clouds
and sail us on the sea.

This feels good,
it's free falling
in perfect harmony.

This feels good,
it's a hypnotic castle
with sand dunes as a moat.

This feels good,
it's walk on air,
it's watch us as we float.

This feels good,
it's a sweet melodic rhythm
gently sweeping through the night.

This feels good,
it's silky and it's sensual,
it's bathed in candlelight.

This feels good,
it's special served on special
at destiny's desire.

This feels good,
it's chip cookie cocktails
served by a roaring fire.

This feels good,
it's an embroidered chair,
caressed by the amber glow.

This feels good,
It's now time, it's our time,
It's - 'please go slow'.

This feels good,
it's cosy, it's warm,
it's spiritually free.

This feels good,
it's a taste of loving,
it's you are here with me.

Brief Encounter
By Jools Coggon

Their reluctant parting.
A time warp conceded.
An arrangement half made
for their next meeting.
Surprised thoughts
absorbed her journey home.

'Two weeks seems too long now.
Though he didn't say so'
And 'hey you. Go steady
with your troubled past.
He's temptation personified.
Who needs it!?'

But no..
Words left unspoken..
Egoless. Sensitive. Different. Appealing.
And the kiss.. unexpected.. nice!
Her aching all night
for the closeness of touch.
Just hand meeting hand -
She'd needed that much.

And then the dream..
She was flying, as often.
Graceful on air.
Effortless movement. Picking up pace.
Weightless sensation. Anticipation.
Then there, on the cloud,
she pictured his face.

Love is all
By Kelly Sweet

Love is all

Love is indefinable
Unbelievable
Inconceivable

Love is fluid
Fickle
Wicked

Love is mysterious
Mischievous
Delirious

Love is passionate
Compassionate
Dispassionate

Love is enveloping
Developing
Revolving

Love is breathing
Conceiving
Bereaving

Love is humour
Laughter
Stupor

Love is madness
Kindness
Blindness

Love is all

Fourteen Love
By Kelly Sweet

Forgotten? Never! Forsaken? Perhaps.
Four years of significance
Strong feelings have lapsed
We were so young.

As nature has cycles
And Seasons have time
We had our innocence
And pretence was sublime.

Our balance was perfect
Our thoughts were entwined
Hearts racing in tandem
'Love' always so blind.

Four years to awaken
To the obvious truth
Life hands out tricks
to all naive youth.

Decay
By Lloyd Williams

Well here we are again. Alone in a room together with nothing to say.

So we sit in silence without even the pretence of caring anymore, without any effort to fill our empty ears with junk so that we might feel normal, even if only for a minute or two.

I could ask how your day went but I don't care to ask like you don't care to tell, so I don't. I just sit, and stare ahead, trying to conceal the contempt building up inside because of your very presence. It's not your fault any more than mine. It's ours, plural.

Every move you make annoys and I know lying next to you later will leave me feeling empty, our bed a coffin for a dead relationship.
It was healthy once and fulfilling, brought joy and contentment. Now it's rotten and consuming, its metabolism was too fast for us, its hunger has turned on us and we're consumed day by day.

Funny how a relationship can turn like that. We thought it was ours, our love, but it was beyond our control. We were out of our depth, and now we're an inch from drowning.

Nice to Remember
By Lydia Millslow

Today I flipped the mattress on my bed and found a forgotten forget-me-not from yesteryear.

For the longest time it had been hidden, stowed away for safekeeping and eventually lost from memory.

My heart stopped when it caught my eye, like the first time I saw it, left on the dresser as a surprise upon waking.

Anticipation of the words written on this scrap of paper swelled through me. I did nothing for a few moments but stare as my mind returned to that time past.

The smells and tastes lingered. Words echoed and touches caressed once more.

I took the letter, one of love no doubt, and it felt vulnerable between my fingers, like dried tissue after soaking. I hardly dared open it in case it crumbled, finally lost forever before I could read it once more.

Gentle, like creeping, I opened the sheet and years old creases flexed again, resurrected. Daylight illuminated the words written and they read as though penned yesterday.

To be told again, after all these years, how precious I am, how loved and desired, made me brim and to be sure I blushed. I remembered his hand and imagined how it looked as he wrote. I imagined the look on his face as he declared his love in writing.

I would have clutched the paper to my chest if I could have taken my eyes from it.

The smile on my face grew on third and fourth readings because I thought of the hug I gave him when next I saw him, the kiss I placed on the tip of his nose. The light in his eyes filled me and the world felt right.

Of course things changed. Our love, like his letter, was forgotten and eventually faded. These words were written a lifetime ago and the feelings behind them have so long ago faded.
Still.
It was nice to remember.

Autumn Wedding
By Maggie Huscroft

We will have an autumn wedding,
Not for us spring's giddy green.
We will have more mellow sunlight
And the harvest coming home.

The young are welcome to the springtime,
With all its Hey Ho! Nonny No!
We will feast beside the fire
Basking in its gentle glow.

Not for us the wicked August,
Nor the rougher winds of May,
We will have the fruits of autumn
Winter's store of summer sun.

Refuge
By Maggie Huscroft

Wonder that this
book of life
was written
in the summer sun.
Seasons change
And colours fade.
Shadows shift to show
a lifetime in her eyes
and winter in her hair.
He reaches out
to take her hand,
and in her face
he sees a land,
a place
where he can take
his ease.
For spring
waits for him there.

My Rock
By Mike Lucas

It is at times when I am away from you,
That I realise that all you have given to me is mine to keep.
And all that you have taken will always be shared,
Though it is gladly yours forever.

It is at times when you are not near to me,
That the fear of not saying what is on my mind holds such a
    voice.
And all of the words that you have spoken bring me peace,
Though I long for them once more.

It is at times when you are out of reach,
That I long to lay beside you and hold you close.
And every touch that you have laid upon my skin returns to me
    and warms me,
Though the feeling may bring me tears.

It is at times when I cannot see your face,
That I am forever thankful for your beauty within my life,
And every expression, whether of sadness or of joy keeps you
    within my heart,
Though it never ceases to ache for your return.

It is at times when the memories and the truth come closer than
the pain of the world,
That I know that we have made the right choices and we are
each other's.
And all that we have made between us is more beautiful than
each of us,
And will always be our blessing.

It is at times when we are together,
That I wish that I could speak as I write.
And let you know that without you and what you have given to
me, I amount to nothing,
Though with you in my heart and my mind I forever have you
beside me.

Without regret, without jealousy, without dreams.
For, as I travel throughout life and across land,
You are my light and you are my rock
That will forever bring me home.

Light of Life
By Paula Beeton

The eyes have it. No!, wait, could it be..
It's the crooked smile that does it for me
The smile is in your eyes though
It lights up your face.
Takes me to another time. A better place.

You light up the day and warm the cold night
To be in your arms is heaven...safe haven
Makes me feel loved, makes the world right
Even in darkness you bring me the light
Takes me to another time. A better place

How could it have been right before?
Before my knowing you I found my way
Yet I stumbled through night, thinking it day
I was blind to what that light could be
You are my day, my night. You are the light.

Out of the darkness
By Paula Beeton

You are the light that came out of the darkness
You are the light that drew me as a moth to the flame
You are the light that warmed my heart
My life will never be the same. With you, without you
My life will never be the same.

You are the joy which fills my heart
Sometimes the sorrow which rends it apart
You are the very core of my wretched being
My life will never be the same. With you, without you
My life will never be the same

You shape my days, my thoughts, my nights
I cannot act or think, or simply be
Without your spirit to love and guide and nurture
My life will never be the same. With you, without you
My life will never be the same.

What were the days before you brought your light?
How did I fill that void? It was through fog I walked
Stumbled from day to night to day, and on again. Blindly
My life will never be the same. With you, without you
My life will never be the same.

You brought with you joy and empathy and hope
You brought laughter and tears, a will to cope
You opened my eyes to who I was. To who I am
My life will never be the same. With you, without you
My life will never be the same.

Mostly you brought me love to have and keep
I sometimes tossed it back. Puzzled, wary
You bounce it back again. You are my rock
My life will never be the same. With you, without you
My life will never be the same.

My door is open now. Unwary am I, bathed in your love
I take your heart gift as you took mine. Yet uncertain
Together we will walk brave into the light
My life will never be the same. With you, without you
My life will never be the same.

Love is come. Love is hope and joy
Love is sorrow and angry and happy and blind
Love is forever and beyond. In death as in life
My life will never be the same. With you, without you
My life will never be the same.

The Girl of his Dreams
By Penny Graham

Robert had seen the girl of his dreams several times. She worked in the public library and he knew she was a local girl because of her accent. A local lad himself, he was proud of knowing his way round town and so he decided to ask her out.

But shyness clamped his tongue to the roof of his mouth, like a car parked in the wrong place but now unable to release itself to the right place.

"Do…do…" he stammered and fled in confusion.

Thus thwarted, his love never developed beyond being a beautiful dream. Eventually the hope of what-might-be became no more than a wild memory of what-might-have-been.

Until the day she walked through the swing doors, her thick lustrous hair falling in waves round her face in exactly the way it always used to. Robert forgot the public library had been closed for some time due to lack of funding. He forgot the years of unrequited longing and spoke at last.

"Doreen," he cried, full of love and joy. "I've been waiting so long for you and at last here you are!"

The girl looked at Robert with a mix of apprehension and pity. What she had heard was,

"Do-o ee, beno wa'er lolo hehe arr!"

Embarrassed, she appealed to the care assistant who was busy extricating the dodgy footrest of Robert's wheelchair from the ball of knitting wool that had fallen off the lap of the wispy-haired elderly lady dozing by the window and unravelled itself all the way across the room.

"I've come to visit my granny, Doreen Dudley," she said.

"That's right, we were expecting you," smiled the carer. "I'll just tell her you're here." She tapped the elderly lady gently on the shoulder. "Wake up, Doreen," she said, "your granddaughter's here."

"Do-o ee!" cried Robert. "Oo eer?"

Just then his kindly ex-neighbour came back into the sitting room. She had been enjoying a confidential chat with the manager of the nursing home about whether a course of speech therapy might help improve his speech which had become difficult to understand since his stroke the year before. She couldn't help thinking it sounded as if his tongue was permanently clamped to the roof of his mouth.

"Is there anything you want me to bring you next time I come?" she asked brightly, as she always did to indicate the visit was over.

'No, thank you, there's nothing I need, unless you see some of those chocolate biscuits I like when you're doing your shopping,' was what Robert wanted to say. What he actually said was,

"Do-o ee, oo eer!"

Doreen blinked herself awake, saw her granddaughter carefully rewinding the ball of wool and thought again how much she resembled herself when young.

"Cep' I was even prettier,' she thought smugly.

"'Ave you brought me those choccy biccies I wanted?" she demanded. "Well, you give 'em 'ere then. I don't want that old man in the wheelchair getting 'is 'ands on 'em."

Terms and Conditions
By Penny Graham

Sometimes she wished she'd made a different decision. Said no, instead of the "um, uh" which had been taken as assent. But because it was very unlikely she would ever be called on to fulfil the commitment she'd agreed to almost by default, she left it in abeyance assuming the whole idea would gather dust somewhere in the forgotten corners of their lives.

But her brother and sister-in-law hadn't let the idea gather dust. They discussed her less than enthusiastic response but in the end felt it would be irresponsible to do nothing, although they too thought it was very unlikely the guardianship would ever need to be invoked.

The day of the accident was an unseasonably warm Saturday and when the news came, she was methodically weeding the garden and mulling over her plans for the summer. These included a long-awaited trip to America and the possibility of trading in her serviceable but boring hatchback for something a bit more exciting and zippy. Now, if ever she dared look back, the confusion of events of the next few weeks seemed like a series of cuttings in a scrapbook no one had yet had the time to put into sequence.

It was only now that she was, literally, coming to terms with it all. The terms were, as well as the obvious ones of no holiday, no new car and loss of job and independence, that she had to stop protesting her unsuitability for surrogate motherhood.

"Why do you want to adopt him?" asked the social worker and she wondered if it was only her imagination that sensed a genuine personal interest behind the official interrogation. Why did she want to adopt her orphaned nephew, when her side of the conditions was that she already enjoyed all the responsibilities and rights of his legal guardian for the next eighteen years, give or take the last few months?

Rain lashed against the window, promising an early start to winter. From upstairs, the baby's thin wail cut into her thoughts, making her completely forget the high-minded and slightly sentimental speech she'd thought she ought to prepare in anticipation of the question. Apologising to the social worker, she got up to see to the baby, then remembered she still hadn't answered.

"I love him," she said.

Live Love
By Rebecca Adams

So you don't know what love is?
Hey - we all don't know what love is.
Emotion is emotive,
but we all live to be loved.

I'm tempted to tell you.
Tempted to know you.
Tempted to show you.
We all live to be loved.

When we cannot express love,
we should work at our expression,
love needs to be nurtured,
we all lived to be loved.

We all live to be loved.
We all live to be loved.
It's the answer to life's question.
We all live to be loved.

If you're higher now than before.
If you need to know the score.
Guess you'd like it if I'd show you
how it is to be loved.

I'm tempted to tell you.
Tempted to show you.
Tempted to know you.
We all live to be loved.

When all reason's without meaning.
When the canvas is thin air,
When the picture's lost its focus.
We all need to be loved.

We all live to be loved.
We all live to be loved.
It's the answer to all searching.
We all live to be loved.

If your heart is crying out now.
If belonging means more.
Then wisdom is in knowing,
we all lived to be loved.

I'm tempted to tell you.
Tempted to know you.
Tempted to show you.
We all live to be loved.

If you ever feel love,
Don't worry that it's not 'real love'.
Fear of love's too empty,
we all live to be loved.

We all live to be loved.
We all live to be loved.
It's the answer to all yearning.
We all live to be loved.

So you don't know what love is?
Hey - we all don't know what love is.
Emotion is emotive,
but we all love to be loved.

Head over heels in love
By Ruth Birch

We have reached that stage of donning vests,
Doing jigsaws, wearing spectacles.
But that doesn't prevent us making a spectacle of ourselves.
Dancing until we can hardly stand, kissing in public, walking
   hand in hand.
You have to hand it to us; we're head over heels in love.

We have reached that stage where there is no better company
Than our own. Just the two of us together. Comfortable in all we do.
But that doesn't prevent us from sampling all that's new.
New restaurants, new bars, new dishes, new locations.
You'll locate us there together. We're head over heels in love.

We have reached that stage where the latest hits
Don't necessarily feature in our CD racks. But sometimes they do.
We do what we like. Listen to music because it pleases.
Wear the fashion that suits us. We have that confidence
That comes from being head over heels in love.

We have reached that stage, let's not call it age
Where a night in is more perfect than a night out.
Where we prefer to be with our family and friends
Than to be forever searching for entertainment.
A different outlook, but we're still head over heels in love.

Parallel Lives
By Sally Edwards

I live a double life, double love life, both existing together, sometimes parallel, occasionally overlapping. I've spent years chasing the memory of Joe, whilst still living a perfectly normal exterior life, my emotional arena has been in constant shift, sometimes in the now, often in the past or an imagined possible future, the one where I find Joe again.

Memory is a wonderful thing. Like a shadow reflected along the path, longer where it shouldn't be, reflecting things bigger than they are. Then with the sun behind a cloud, gone; the path smudgy grey with the left behind scuff marks from wheeling bikers.

My recollection of Joe is grainy, certain things clear as a summer day, and others fogged with passed time. The hint of a certain cologne sends my head spinning back to the time when the weatherman forgot to tell us about an up coming hurricane and the unforgettable night that followed. The shadow of a candle lit face in a bar, cigarette in hand, smoke obscuring the eyes sets my heart racing in the hope of a fateful chance meeting sending us off again on that wild tangent that was our romance.

Crowded places offer me a million opportunities in countless faces to see him again, the swing of a raincoat or the sound of a voice could all be him. Trips to London offer tantalising half glimpses of my nearly-Joes as I search every upward and downward approaching face on the underground escalators, never giving up on the idea that I'll get lucky, hoping that this time he might be there, destiny offering that crucial reunion.

If a person's really looking it's amazing how many could - be places there are to find someone. I know I'll find him. Just as fate initially crossed our paths, so fate will offer us that same chance again.

I imagine my heart to be tattooed with a thousand million little initials, like school kids draw on their desk - JP luvs SE. Each heart beat reverberating the love, echoing the pattern of our initials on and on, just like my search for Joe, goes on and on.

When I find him again, all I want to do is hold him, ask him if he can find it in his heart to love me again. Tell him that I've stopped settling for second best, and that I was a fool to ever think that he was anything else but the best.

I am propelled by the hope that his heart beats to the same rhythm as mine, and that when fate crosses our paths we can make a better job of it than last time. And until then, I carry on with my parallel life, heart beating in two directions at once.

A fine line between love and hate
By Sally Edwards

Each scream is a flattening of my soul, rupturing the connection to myself, leaving my soul a little bit more depleted.

Whilst on the outside I say, "Good boy for eating your sandwich," teeth gritted, eyes smiling -but not. Faced with the knowing stare of my child who screams again, and it begins again.

At the end of the day I collapse in a heap, stretched, ironed out, flattened by the constant and never ending demands of my children. I crumple in front of the TV, trying to refill my soul with films devoid of character and chocolate lacking the life giving lustre I seek. Stuffing myself to oblivion, hoping to fill my soul again, till the onslaught begins again the next day.

So it goes on, this motherhood cycle, want, want, want all day: give, give, give; and myself given up in meeting the constant ego demands of my offspring.

I feel myself disappearing in the process. I try hanging onto a bit of me, but I've forgotten in my sleep starved, catatonic state what me ever was. What I looked like or felt like. With the next scream a wisp of me disappears into the ether, lost again. I wonder if there's a place in heaven where I'll be able to pick up the lost and forgotten remnants of myself. I just wonder if I'll recognise them or need them by then.

Being a mother is like a sort of subtle Chinese Water torture – drip, drip, drip: want, want, want. Not only did I lose my figure, but some days I feel like I'm losing my mind too.

It's a fine line between love and hate. I love my children. But there are days when I hate them too. The thought flashes through my mind as I bath them, hardly visible, like a sunbeam glancing off a dewdrop. I swoop them up in my arms, drop a guilt edged kiss on their heads, and hope they can't read my mind.

This pendulum of love and hate swings through my mind, resting like a veil over my thoughts sending me into flurries of anxiety driven action and play dates. The children watch with wide eyes wondering what's coming next.

I'm just hanging on, hoping for good days to get me through the bad ones. Knowing that a scream can swing mother love to mother hate in the time it takes a sandwich to be thrown to the floor.

That Special Day?
By Sheila Cameron

The day was set excitement grew,
their wedding day was here.
The cars arriving, men in suits
and some the worse for beer.
Aunt Beryl in her silly hat
and limping with her gout.
Dear cousin Cheryl with her 'boobs'-
guests also spilling out!
Uncle Bert and Auntie May
the list went on and on.
I thought that most of them were dead,
had upped their toes and gone!
The bride and groom looked scared, withdrawn,
with people's constant touch.
The oohs and ahhs, and aren't they cute
just made them lick their crutch.
Yap! only in the USA
they'd dress up in their togs.
Whose daft idea and money gain
to wed the b...dy dogs!

Love Among the Pebbles
By Sheila Cameron

I need to make you mine. In time
I will return, you'll learn, that love's unending
journey, makes us yearn to spend the years as one.
I'd take the sun and shine it - twine it
on the beach of shiny pebbles.
Take the pebble - keep it with you,
may it give you my devoted love.
Make our pebbles kiss; now they'll
return together. Pretty Miss
please promise me, they'll
tether our love, weather all the woes
before me.
He stood.
My handsome hero kissed in love,
leaving me on that beach.
I stroked the pebble, knew we'd treble
unending love on his return.
He took his beret, shone the badge
with pride.
He died.
My young dear love.
Above, he looks down on that beach,
so many pebbles - out of reach.

Our Love Boat
By Sheila Cameron

We took our boat far out to sea,
the day was fresh, the air was clean.
Our life beginning, sun kissed love,
the brightest day we'd ever seen.
Little boat with engine pumping,
soft wind blowing through my hair.
So excited – two hearts together,
thanking God that he was there.
Calm blue sea with small waves rippling,
we could hardly see the shore,
wanted just to be beside him
this day, and so many more.
Pumping engine coughed and spluttered,
he just sighed, we laughed.
In love we hardly noticed. Now saw danger
sent a flare, it rose above.
High in the sky of blue - flare red,
but blue went grey - and quick a haze.
I felt his nervous apprehension
as swirling mist - heads in a daze.
He held me in his arms so tightly,
felt assured, but senses tight.
Handsome Prince, please save your maiden
close the book, and make it right.
The coastline disappeared before us.

Our perfect day? I prayed inside.
The dissipated flare now distant,
Would fate come and turn the tide?
Drifting, waves increasing stronger
boat now rocking - then violently bobbing
buffeting, our every meaning.
Our life ebbing - my soul sobbing.
Noone listening to my crying
he in pain from falling – listless,
calming words I tried to sooth him.
Now his body feeling lifeless.
In my arms my turn to hold him,
my heart yearning me to save,
don't take away my soul forever,
and leave him to this watery grave.
Through the mist I heard a warning.
Loud ship's noises, voices yell.
Strong arms lift through mist to safety,
saved us from the seaside hell.
Twelve years on I sit in silence.
Memories haunt me like a slave.
Will his cold hand ever leave me?
Walking past his piteous grave.

Family
By Sheila Cameron

It's fun being mum feeling one
with your son as a chum,
daughter too as a mate, both are great!
And your love as a mother like no other
feelings match when they hatch good as new
just for you, and their dad
has a lad and a girl, feelings whirl in your head,
fears and dread.
make them safe, keep them strong.
Get it wrong, like you will - love them still
always, ever rougher weather
may appear hold them near,
not all rosy? make it cosy!
Cook their dinner, you're a winner!
On their own, they leave home.
Back they come, always to Mum.

My Fairground
By Sheila Cameron

I paid my fare and took my chance,
a young new bride
I loved the dance,
the merry go round with you a thrill
together in a trance.
From ride to ride we ran through life
on bumps and spins -
a mother - wife.
Our children grew and left the nest
felt lonely full of strife.
The roundabout began to slow
that rush of love
I couldn't show,
but your love just as strong, I knew
I had to let you know.
The look of pain that creased your face
your hurt inside.
Please give me space!
My helter skelter ride had stopped
no longer in your place.
I wander round the fairground now
a lonely soul -
my thoughts allow
deep feelings – fears to realise
I am without you now.

Ol' Whiskey Breath
By Stuart Johnson

Ol' whiskey breath, you look like death
I take it she's left you again
Taken the kid, and your last shiny quid
Now you're staggering about in the rain
I told you to choose, between her and the booze
Looks like you took the wrong turning
Now she's filed for divorce, wants everything of course
What lessons are you learning?
Not many it seems, same impossible dreams
Went double or quits on the horses
Now you're going full throttle, with your half-empty bottle
Draining the Earth's alcohol resources

Ol' whiskey breath, more than a hair's breadth
From the reality of your situation
You say it's cool, tomorrow she'll call
But the poison's got you taking dictation
Now you seek a quick solution, a fast-love absolution
A painted face who trades it on the street
But you're way beyond discerning, take another wrongful
    turning
And now you're mixing with a different kind of meat
This is where I apprehend, though you used to be a friend
I must take you by the arm and lead you home
Before you sink much deeper, I must ask as head zoo-keeper
That you leave that bloody chimpanzee alone.

False Teethmarks
By Stuart Johnson

You cannot say I didn't try
To keep our fires burning
To stoke them once before we die
And awaken dormant yearnings
On our 70th anniversary
Thought I'd inject a little spice
Your reaction was less than cursory
When I said that you looked nice
I nibbled at your hairy ears
I even used my tongue
But instead you put the kettle on
And switched on Jimmy Young
So I chased you to the kitchen
To try and keep things on the simmer
But it took me nearly half an hour
To reach you with my Zimmer
I said "Come now my withering buttercup"
"How about one last piece of action?"
"Have you eaten all the biscuits again?!"
Was not the desired reaction
And so you left me with no choice
I had to implement Plan B
Though perhaps Plan Z is a little more apt
When you're pushing ninety-three
I had to stir your fading memories

And rekindle past adventures
So I took the plunge
With an unsteady lunge
I ripped your bra off with my dentures
Just like that time in 1935
Waiting for that train at Coulsdon South
Of course it seemed far sexier then
When the teeth were still in my mouth

Teethmarks
By Stuart Johnson

I remember the peaceful delirium
Of rising, swooping, soaring
Through the hazy Niagara air
Relentless, twirling blades above me
The merciless, thundering falls below
Crashing foamy white maelstroms
I remember thinking to myself
There can be no-one out there
That could match this wonder of nature
That could drown your orientation
That could wash you out to oblivion
With such rampaging velocity
But I had no clue that Fate was scheming
And had perched you on the approaching horizon
Liked a cursed figurine on a mantelpiece
Ready to ensnare me with those dark and pretty eyes
Short black rock chick hair and curved Italian smile
We met, we acknowledged and we talked
Could not have foreseen we'd grow so close
So close and yet so far
That I'd draw such envious glances
In bars and clubs filled with the blend of smoke and testosterone
Those Saturday night male egos would never know
That you and I were not to be

That you were the merciless thundering falls

That I was sealed inside a barrel, floating towards the edge

Unable to swim away from the foaming precipice

And on drunken taxi rides home

You'd rest your head on my shoulder

You'd tell the driver I was the brother you'd never had

And I knew then, I knew that it was over

And I knew then that it had never begun

Four years on, unannounced and uninvited

You invade my sleep, trespass in my dreams

I rise and swoop above you

As you rage and crash below

And all I have are teethmarks

I wear your teethmarks on my heart

I wear them on my soul

Invisible

Slow to heal

Mr and Mrs Nnngff and the
Time Travelling Confession Box
By Stuart Johnson

I went for a spin the other day in Father McCready's confession box.

The catalyst was our seventh pint of the black stuff down at our local. We were indulging in our usual friendly debate over the moral issue of the day, and on this occasion the subject was marriage.

"Marriage," I said, "is outdated. Marriage mostly was, is, and always will be doomed to failure. Marriage is as futile and pointless as asking Naomi Campbell to give you a hand with the Sunday Times crossword. "

"Nonsense my son," Father McCready replied. "And what's more, I shall prove that it's nonsense. Come back to the church with me and I'll prove that marriage can work in any place, at any time."

I knew what he was referring to here. It had been rumoured for some time that Father McCready had mastered the phenomena of time travel. Furthermore, it had been said he'd overseen numerous famous marriage ceremonies, including Monroe and DiMaggio, Bogart and Bacall and er....Paul Daniels and Debbie McGee.

As we staggered back to the church, he admitted the upcoming exercise would kill two birds for him. He told me he'd always wanted to conduct the very first marriage ceremony in history, chronologically.

We took our seats in the confession box, and I watched in awe as the dial span backwards through time.... "Five thousand years".... "Ten thousand".... until it finally came to rest at "Pre-Barbara Cartland".

We stepped outside.

"Perfect!" cried McCready, "Over there." He pointed towards a cave up ahead, standard three-bedroom semi-detached with en-suite twigs and a poorly laid driveway.

Stood at the entrance in an aggressive stance were two figures. Cro-Magnon, one male and one female. Neither of whom seemed overly happy to see us.

"Hello," McCready called over to them, picking his way across the uneven ground. A small rock flew over his head.

"Nnngff," replied the male, which I think translated as "Go away or I will kill you."

I stopped at a safe distance as the Priest approached undeterred.

"Hello, my name is Father McCready, do-you-have-names?" He asked slowly.

"Nnngff," said cavewoman.

"Nnngff," shouted caveman.

"Marvellous, well without further ado, I shall perform the ceremony." He removed a pink carnation from his coat pocket and placed it in the female's hair. As he strode back towards me, the nonplussed female picked the flower from her straggly hair, examined it.... and then ate it.

"Mr Nnngff, do you take Mrs Nnngff to be your lawful wedded wife?"

"Nnngff!"

"And Mrs Nnngff..." we both dodged a wooden spear, "...do you take Mr Nnngff to be your lawful wedded husband?"

"Nnngff."

"I now pronounce you man and wife. You may kiss the bride."

"Nnngff?" The male looked confused.

"Oh...er..." McCready pointed at his own pouting lips and then at the female.

The male grunted, picked up a rock and smashed it in his newly-wed's face. The female screamed and inspected the blood on her fingers. She then picked up the rock and smashed it in the male's tender regions.

"There you go Father," I said. "Proof that marriage never works. They'll be filing for divorce within the hour."

"Nonsense," he replied as we watched the male hopping about in agony, clutching his groin. "Merely a mutual decision on their part not to have children. That was a neolithic vasectomy."

As the 'domestic' descended into further violence, we decided to beat a hasty retreat.

Mister Seventh Time Lucky
By Stuart Johnson

The twenty-eighth day of the first month, the year 1547.

At the gates, Saint Peter had no real clue to dates and times, so the significance of this day in Western Europe was lost on him. Had he known, he wouldn't have given a Serpent's backside about it anyway.

The sound of approaching footsteps through the thick mist spurred him into action, and he secreted his copy of What Pitchfork? beneath his robes, aware that the 'boss' could be prone to directorial visits at any time.

When the figure appeared it had a beard alright, but to Saint Peter's relief this was a short ginger one rather than a long flowing white one.

The beard was attached to a bloated face, nestled above a portly frame dressed in badly soiled bed-clothes.

"Don't we know you?" Peter asked.

"Should do," Ginger replied, "Certainly made my mark."

"Name?"

"Henry."

"Last name?"

"Err.....The Eighth."

"Right bear with me Mister Err The Eighth."

Peter began unravelling his scroll of names. It took him two weeks.

"Ah... " he said eventually. "....Oh...oh yes, we know about you don't we?...uh-huh, six wives..." He tutted, trailing a finger down the scroll, "...mm, a couple of divorces in there..."

The Tudor King shuffled from one foot to the other.

"Well?"

"Well it's not looking great is it Henry, my old mucker?"

"You're not going to let me in are you?"

"Henry...." Peter scratched his head, "Tell me about Love. "

"About what?"

"Not your strong point I realise, but tell me about love. And I don't mean a quick 'wham-bam thank you ma'am, chopping block's over there' type of love....I'm talking about Luurrrve." Peter did a quick grind of the hips and snogged the palm of his hand.

Henry looked baffled.

"Okay," said Peter, "Let's gloss over your misdemeanours down below. What can you offer us here in Heaven? What are you looking for here?"

"A wife."

"What? Another one?!"

"I still need a wife who can bear me a son."

Saint Peter regarded the fallen King, almost sympathising with his desperation.

"But Henry, I'm rather afraid that can't happen now. We could provide you with a spiritual wife maybe, but you couldn't copulate with her because you are dead, and she couldn't reproduce because she is dead."

"Well, what use would she be to me then?"

"It brings us back to the question of 'Love' Henry."

"I still don't know what you mean by that word."

"It would have to be a spiritual marriage if we gave you a wife here. Nothing more than companionship and respect. You would have to love her, purely for who she is. This is the land of the departed, Henry. You can't divorce the deceased, or behead the dead."

"Well," the King shrugged and sighed. "Thanks but I er... I think I'd better leave it."

"Where are you going?" Peter asked. He kind of liked this guy.

"I'll have to give the other place a try."

Disentanglement
By Stuart Johnson

"Please don't say that. "

"Say what, Michael? "

"Do not insult my intelligence with the I didn't know pretence. You've always known how I felt about you. "

"Where is this coming from? " Rebecca poured herself an orange juice, and whisked the dark hair away from her eyes as she curled herself up on the sofa. "Michael...you and me...we're friends yeah? I mean, good friends right? "

She didn't need this kind of potentially melodramatic conversation with a man. Certainly not at eight in the morning when she was more concerned about going to work.

Michael remained silent..

"Okay, " she conceded, " Yeah, I had an idea you had a soft spot for me..."

"A soft spot? " Michael was incredulous.

"But what can I do? I've never seen us that way, I'm sorry. You're a lovely bloke, but..."

There was nothing shattering about Rebecca's words. He'd realized for sometime that these feelings, these crippling emotions were his, and his alone.

"Got what you needed out of the situation though didn't you? " He pursed his lips in grim appraisal.

"What do you mean? "

"Good old Michael eh? Good old Michael will take me down the club and pay for me to get in. Good old Michael will buy my drinks for me, and listen to my troubles. How could he refuse..."

"No, that's not true... "

"And by the way, I know that money I lent you was spent on cocaine. Every fifteen minutes disappearing to the toilets…"

Rebecca snapped and slammed her glass down on the coffee table.

"Okay if you want the truth, here's the truth! Yes I played you for the pathetic thing that you are. You're too easy, too convenient and too… too nice! For gods sake what's wrong with you! Dance with somebody else now and again, find somebody else to fall in love with. "

"You don't understand. " Michael said quietly.

"What don't I understand? "

"It really doesn't matter anymore. I've been so tangled up in you, everything about you, but now I'm going to disentangle myself and you're about to realise. "

"Realise what Michael? Bloody hell, just move on will you. Be a man about it. "

"Oh don't worry babe, I'm about to do something that's gonna rock your world. The kind of exciting act you thought I wasn't up to. "

"What are you talking about? "

Michael stood calmly for a moment on the ledge of his twelfth floor apartment, staring downwards.

"Well…It might rock your world….either that, or it'll leave you searching for absolution. " He swiped a tear from his cheek with his sleeve. "But for me…release, amnesty, disentanglement. "

"Michael, what are you babbling about. "

"Goodbye gorgeous. " He carefully placed his phone down on the ledge.

"Michael?......Michael, what are you doing?.............Michael?"

I Would Follow The Jetstreams
By Stuart Johnson

Old enough to know you were not coming back
Too young to understand, or know how to react
But the holes still appear, homing in for the kill
Gaping ever wider and quicker than I can fill
With empty jokes and distant smiles
My inside and outside never quite reconciled
Give me one final chance, a belated shot
At knowing a father who was removed from the plot
I crave a reunion with your ethereal ghost
To replace vague memories I half-heartedly toast
Please lay me a trap, or provide me a map
Turn the wind on my face and show me the signs
As I would follow the currents, follow the treelines
Show me you're out there, and I will remain calm
And I will follow the jetstreams to return to your arms

The Night The Arrows Flew No More
By Stuart Johnson

"Am I a police officer or a samaritan? Why do I get lumbered with this? "

"Dunno Sarge," Constable Pooley spat egg sandwich across the dashboard. "Guess you must have a sympathetic face."

"The only sympathy I have is for the poor bastard who has to fish his body out the river. Not that he'll actually jump of course - they never do. Get his fifteen minutes of attention and then back home to his semi-detached."

"Oh well, enjoy. Break a leg."

"I'll do more than break their leg, push the time-waster into the river myself."

Sergeant Cooper ducked under the cordon and strode up to the officer already on site.

"Right, what we got this time? Drama queen? Tortured soul? Or is this one really gonna take the plunge?"

"Um, it sounds pretty determined sir." The young officer wore a pale, spooked expression.

"It? What do you mean It?"

The officer just shrugged, mystified.

"Him...her...it..." Cooper muttered away at himself, hugging his coat around himself as he walked out to the centre of the bridge, "...Don't care what it bloody is, it's got five minutes and then.....oh..."

He stopped. Blinked furiously as he tried to comprehend his subject.

Cooper had reason to be moody and bad-tempered. He was above most of what he had to deal with.

Cultured and educated. A big fan of Greek and Roman mythology among other things.

"Oh," he said again. " So it's you."

The It in question was technically a he. Sat precariously on the edge of mortality.

The wings were tangled, riddled with mould. Naked of course, true to the myth, but unshaven with a world weary look in his eyes. Scattered on the ground next to him lay a bow and several arrows, long devoid of any radiant glow that might once have surrounded them. Now rotting away, rusting.

"You know who I am then?" He croaked with surprise, raising a bottle of Bells to his lips.

"Of course. I know who you are. But what happened to you? And why end it? Why now?"

Cupid, for it was he of course, finished the last of the whiskey.

"My work is done," he replied. "I gave it my best shot... if you'll scuse the pun."

"I don't understand."

"True love is dead. Romance is dead. Look around you. Divorce rates, domestic abuse, sordid affairs, internet pornography when the wife's away, teenage pregnancies, Burberry nappies and casual sex rife amongst the masses. You people disgust me."

"But.... "

"Love is something you buy nowadays, not something you feel. As for romance..." Cupid scoffed dismissively, " A Burger King meal in front of Eastenders, there's your modern ideal of romance."

The mythical amoretto braced for the jump.

"We're not all like that," Cooper blurted desperately. "I'm happily married."

"Your wife's sleeping with your brother."

"What!"

"And your daughter had an abortion last month."

"My daughter? She's fourteen!"

"Yep. That's the one."

Cooper watched dumbstruck as Cupid splashed into the dark waters below.

From Bliss To Hiss
By Stuart Johnson

We awoke to the warming sun draping itself lazily across our bodies, tangled amongst the bed-clothes.

Contentment.

No, this was more than contentment.

Bliss...yes that was it.

Susan was the one, I'd known that from the moment she'd turned up on my doorstep one morning. The connection had been immediate, and I knew my search was over.

I'd wandered the dampened back streets of Soho, I'd hunted around in the East-end. I knew all the places to look with my dark glasses and my fake moustache. My sinking heart back then could never have foreseen that my longing for a particular romance would end like this.

End in bliss.

I watched her slip into another light doze, my soul swelling with the awe of her beauty.

Perfect soft white skin.

Petite shapely form.

I nestled myself against her and listened to the natural tranquillity of the morning.

"Are you as happy as me? " I whispered into her shoulder. Not waiting for an answer that might shatter me with disappointment, I turned her head towards me and nodded it for her.

"Susan." It was enough for me just to breathe her name.

I heard the slam of a car door, and it didn't register.

"Susan."

I heard the key turning the lock, and it didn't register.

"Susan."

I heard the front door closing.

"Kathy! Oh shit!... Shit! Shit! Shit!..." I sprung out of bed like a gazelle, scattering blankets and sheets around me, "....Susan, quick sweetheart, I gotta hide you somewhere."

I'd forgotten Kathy was home today.

I grabbed Susan and turned her around, searching frantically for the plastic stopper and yanking it loose.

"Deflate! Deflate, damn you!" I hissed at it, as it hissed itself with agonising apathy.

Footsteps on the stairs.

I pressed at the synthetic material with both hands to hurry it along, the four black legs folding in on the white lumpy body and the black face with the long snout began to shrivel inwards.

"Hello babe! Ohh it's so good to be home." Kathy pecked me on the cheek and collapsed onto the dishevelled bed.

Then she sat up, eyes narrowed.

"What was that?"

"What was what?" I said, frozen to the spot.

"That noise."

"What noise?"

"Sounded like it came from the cupboard.... Sounded like a....'baaaa'... like a.... sheep? God, I've been working too damn hard, that's my problem. "

The Pharaonic Stewardess of EgyptAir 778
By Stuart Johnson

Her high-cheeked beauty, as if sculpted from glass
Mesmerised my soul in economy class
Such dark-eyed promise, my soul she did plunder
As we soared to the land of the ancient wonders
But what passed her lips as she shone down at me?
Just "Coffee or tea?"
Just "Coffee or tea?"

Only reincarnations could be so classically pretty
Could you be Isis, or perhaps Nefertiti
But reality creeps from behind to dishearten
I sure ain't Osiris and I'm no Akhenaten
And your words are rehearsed and detachedly brief
Just "Chicken or beef?"
Just "Chicken or beef?"

If the engines should fail and we crash to the Med
Would you fish out my corpse from the raging sea-bed
And lovingly mummify me with manicured hands
Entomb yourself beside me 'neath Arabian sands
Or just swim down to where my heartbeat grows shorter
With a tray in your hands saying "Orange juice or water?"
"Orange juice or water?"

Descending the steps into the warm Cairo night
My heart slightly dented, your smiles were contrite
And somehow I doubt I'm believing you when
You say "Goodbye, hope to see you again."
Our disparities and backgrounds are hopelessly large
We were just two passing ships in cocooned fuselage
So farewell Nefertiti to your worshipful face
That must surely not belong in my own time and space
So long to your beauty that captured my stare
My Pharaonic stewardess of EgyptAir

REAL BEAUTY
By Sue Frost

When I look at you I see beauty
filled with love for the whole world to see
when you touch me I feel your security
letting me know everything's okay and in time I will see
when you talk to me you deal with reality
non-judgemental, questioning, and challenging, knowing
when to say something and, then when to let it be
when I'm in your arms I know that this was meant to be
the Angels sent you to look after me
I know my mum's watching and she's happy with what she sees
and, she's encouraging us to have the same front door keys
we are just so good together
and everyday our relationship gets better
the openess, the honesty that's shared between the two of us
it's so amazing, I've never known such trust
you are so good for me in so many, many, ways
and, I know I'm good for you and, It's not a passing phase
I look forward when we are together all the time
that's when I'll relax when, I know everything will be fine
until then I send you all my love, plenty of hugs and many
    kisses
and the best of all I send you three wishes
some people would say how could you? It's forbidden fruit
but, the loving is so strong, and together we look so cute.

MY WOMAN'S TOUCH
By Sue Frost

There's nothing more wonderful then a woman's touch
so loving, so caring, so sensitive it really is too much
the feel of your hands on my body turns me wild
the dating game we play makes me act like a child
something so intimate is shared just between you and me
the love so strong for the whole world to see
I feel so relaxed around you
and you make me feel so good, you really do
my heart races, my breathing increases, I don't want this to go
away
I love the way you touch me, and caress me everyday
the passionate hugs make everything seem fine
I think you are so divine
you light up my life and, light up my day
happiness, fun and laughter it's the only way
your touch is such a wonderful thing
you constantly make my heart sing
so I'm just thanking you for coming into my life
together we can and, will survive.

Your Call
By Tanya Withers

Peachy gray, the sky today,
felt my thoughts slide away.
Hit some spot, way back then,
touched your lips, smiled again.
Closed my eyes, drank the air,
could have been anywhere.
Time stands still, for a friend,
hearts don't heal, though they pretend.
Peachy gray, shafts of light,
eerie silence, no-one in sight.
Felt your kiss upon my face,
brings me home, to you, this place.

Love in a Mist
By Tanya Withers

Love in a mist, you get the gist
It's blue as all true love is
Or becomes
In one way or another.
Brother you smother me.
Why can't we be in love
And still feel free
To breathe?

Love-in-a-Mist, cute flowers
but soon die, when cut.
Cut this out. No need to shout
I hear you; fear you, in truth.
Your stifling love is too uncouth
for me.

Love in mist, too crowded
when shrouded with
veiled threats.
You can't live without me?
Honey, try trying.
There's no point in me lying
- I can't love you.

Almost In Love
By Tanya Withers

I am almost in Love with you.
What is this feeling that I try to describe
When I don't really know you
And I don't really understand Love?
It's not lust; I'm not desperate to get you to bed,
Nor to hug or to kiss you.
It's not friendship. I have lots of friends so I know
What that feels like; good, but quite different.
It's not infatuation as I'm not looking for anyone
And I don't want or expect anything from you.
No, it's as I said; I'm almost in Love with you.
It's a heart thing. I feel it. How very strange.

I Am Still
By Tanya Withers

I am still the person
to whom you pledged your love
with tearful eyes and hands
clasped tightly - good actor

I am still the person
to whom you declared undying love
growing, unstoppable, forever,
developing more and more

I am still the person
that you said you loved
when, fists shaking, you pushed
me through your each-way door.

I am still the person
safe-keeping your sincerity
as you back away
when I hit the floor
I am still

Disconnected
By Tanya Withers

Just another lunar cycle

Waxing crescent moon

Shadows of a broken promise

Will you come back soon?

Bye
By Tanya Withers

Same old story.
No glory in it
for either of us.
But will we
let it go?
You know that
you are right.
And I know that
you are wrong.
We could rap
this as our song.
But why bother?
Brother does
it bother you?
Love and passion
grow
into
a blemish.
Same old story.
And the next
line?
Suits me fine.
We go
our separate
ways.

Nirvana tomorrow
By Tony Dew

So what's the problem, rhyming moon
with june sounds good to me (says she)
true nuff (I say) cep tits bin dunna zillion
times before and ain't so fresh. It's
new to me (she says) an di lie kit.

(Goes on) so what's the point,
them's only little lines of
witty, gritty bitsa stuff
that pulls yer bellrope
strokes yer smile.

Yer excercises, same as them
We do in Bible school
xcep we see what's deeper meant,
how every word and every breath
reveals God's intent.

All same pigeon (says I) you know
I'm only trying to make it through t'day
and reach manana. (She) you ain't
gonna let me forget that areya?
Nah but I love yah don't I, kiss me.

Is it love?
By Whetr

I know of this pain, this I know,

Is it love, I hear someone ask?

Takes up my time, do you know?

Is it love, I hear someone ask?

Like lead, it weighs me down,

Wake up, wake up it's reality time,

So someone says, he cares not you clown,

Ouch such pain, all for him whose in the limelight,

A fool for just a bit too long, in this damn town,

Perhaps it's time I looked for a worthier sight.

Love
By Whetr

It is I guess no miracle,
Although it felt like one,
My heart jumped a beat, for a minute I thought it had stopped,
It felt like heaven was smiling at me,
Dashing as ever there he was, as he entered this room with some
   style.
A public meeting and no this was not of some romantic sort,
At long last I saw him, when he came and sat by my side,
It had been nearly 12 years or more, like a story of Mahabaratha,
Perhaps it was I who had been in exile all this while,
As I reflect on the pain and anger , which I can't describe,
Of something that I had lost, of hope, of a future,
Of me once upon a time, perhaps then with a chance,
Did he ever care, I ask? Why did he not call?
Perhaps courting had not been an intention or point.
Did he not want me in his life?
Perhaps it was just a foolish dream.
It's just tears now, Oh why do I cry?
Perhaps he was or is married or gay,
That would be an even lousier luck,
Maybe he had just been a nice guy,
It is such a cruel fate,
To see, yet not to talk, or to touch,
Hurts like nothing before, if only I knew what was wrong,
Was that him, in that car right behind me this time?
My heart raced yet I feared and sped away just the same.

A lagging response, no other attempt at all was his call,
Perhaps it's me and my imaginings, No definitely not,
My intuition can't be wrong.
So acute this pain, so unbearable it's hard to explain.
A pain like nothing I have felt in all my days,
My heart hurts with a yearning I can't describe,
I can no longer cope, as I see him again from time to time,
It feels like a tempting window dressing,
That I am not allowed to enjoy, have, talk to or touch,
Yet I want him day and night by my side,
For the rest of my life and just to be mine,
Without him I think I prefer to die,
This man for some reason captured my heart,
Yet I am scared, of this love, this feeling inside,
Not knowing, how or what he feels, Oh such fears!
I adore him, yet I fear him too, I do not know why,
This was; is 'Andrew' my love lost, perhaps not so after all,
guardian angels guide me now I pray,
If that be so, for my soul mate to be.

I do
By Whetr & K

When you say 'I do', they are not just two words
They are the most powerful thing you will ever say.
For in these three letters a million words are spoken.
They are the voice of the soul, its love to convey.
These small words that tower above skyscrapers.
So simple yet running deeper than the ocean
As the Earth to the Sun, the Moon to the Stars
They are bound in everlasting devotion.
Truer than any blade, they will never bend or corrupt,
They will never be ugly or grow old with time
They are more defiant, more unbreakable than diamond
And their beauty no blindfold can hide.
And I would rather these words than any treasure or earthly
  sum
For their bond is something wealth cannot feign.
When two worlds will collide forever
And from the light, one true love will remain.
So, say 'I do' and change a man into a husband
Say 'I do' and transform a woman into a wife.
For they are the end and they are the beginning.
They are eternity. They are forever. They are for life.

Some definitions of love

1. A score of zero in tennis or squash
2. A strong positive emotion
3. A warm affection
4. Benevolence
5. Sweetheart
6. A deep feeling of sexual desire and attraction
7. An object of warm affection or devotion
8. Delight in /get pleasure from
9. Admire passionately
10. Be enamoured or in love with
11. Have a great affection or liking for
12. Have sexual intercourse with
13. *Become a creative writer – and add your own definition here*

....

www.writebuzz.com has been developed to enable amateur and professional writers to publish and promote their writing, and to provide an exclusive resource for readers. We publish new, imaginative writing, in all genres.

Please visit www.writebuzz.com for a showcase of exciting and inspiring publications by new writers.

Printed in the United Kingdom
by Lightning Source UK Ltd.
131156UK00001B/10-12/P